I'm Good and Other Lies

I'm Good and Other Lies

by Bev Katz Rosenbaum

DCB

 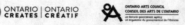

We acknowledge financial support for our publishing activities: the Government of
Canada, through the Canada Book Fund and The Canada Council for the Arts;
the Government of Ontario, through the Ontario Arts Council, Ontario Creates,
and the Ontario Book Publishing Tax Credit. We acknowledge additional funding
provided by the Government of Ontario and the Ontario Arts Council
to address the adverse effects of the novel coronavirus pandemic.

LIBRARY AND ARCHIVES CANADA CATALOGUING IN PUBLICATION

Title: I'm Good and Other Lies / Bev Katz Rosenbaum.
Other titles: I am good and other lies
Names: Rosenbaum, Bev Katz, author.
Identifiers: Canadiana (print) 20210212713 | Canadiana (ebook) 2021021273X |
ISBN 9781770866324 (softcover) | ISBN 9781770866331 (HTML)
Classification: LCC PS8553.R898 I42 2021 | DDC jc813/.54—dc23

United States Library of Congress Control Number: 2021938485

Cover art: Angel Guerra, Archetype
Interior text design: Tannice Goddard, tannicegdesigns.ca

Printed and bound in Canada.
Manufactured by Friesens in Altona, Manitoba in August, 2021.

DCB
AN IMPRINT OF CORMORANT BOOKS INC.
260 SPADINA AVENUE, SUITE 502, TORONTO, ON M5T 2E4
www.dcbyoungreaders.com
www.cormorantbooks.com

This is for everyone who relates to Kelsey Kendler's situation. I hope this book helps you feel a little less alone and a little less hopeless. You are amazing and so very deserving of love.

PART ONE
The Before Times
—

A Fresh Start (Hahahahaha)

1

YEAH, SO THANKS TO my perpetually stoned, unemployable, for-mer comedian mom (for a comic, she's sure a killjoy), we've moved from Toronto's posh Rosedale area to "transitional" Parkdale. It's January and I know absolutely zero persons I'll be at high school with during my last half year of it.

Great, right?

Day One at Queen Street Secondary. Lunch. I paste on a smile and point to an empty chair. "Anybody sitting here?" I ask a pretty but not mean-looking girl who could definitely snag a seat at the popular table if she wanted to, which tells me she's nicer and more down to earth than the girls over there.

"Nope," she says. "Feel free."

Yay! "Thanks," I say, giving her a big (but not too) smile. Once in my seat, I reach into my lunch bag for the tuna sandwich I made last night.

"I'm Molly Jones," Pretty Girl says. "And this is Maddie Tate."

Maddie's face is harder, meaner than Molly's. She gives me a barely perceptible nod.

"Hi, I'm Kelsey. Kendler." I have no idea what else to say. Ugh, I'm way too dressed up. They look dubious.

"Kendler? Are you related to Hannah?" Molly asks.

Now why did I say my last name? My stomach clenches. "Yeah. She's my mom."

"Oh, wow! Must be so great having such a cool mom! Like, actually cool, not *Mean Girls* cool."

I smile at the joke, hoping I don't look too pained.

"I was addicted to *Those Crazy Comics*!" she says. "I'd love to meet her sometime!"

Haha, that'll never happen. Kids of substance misusers (the polite term) don't bring people home. We're basically feral. I had a single friend at my old school: Makayla Cohen, spawn of actress-narcissist Rhonda Silver — we bonded instantly. Makayla's currently in L.A. with Rhonda, and I'm feeling extra blue without her. Not that she loves in-person get-togethers. Doesn't phone or text all that much either. She's an introvert par excellence, happiest when reading books about multiverses or artificial intelligence.

Ugh, why did I think socializing was a good idea?

"She's pretty busy," I finally answer Molly.

Now she's looking at me a bit weirdly. Fab. Now it seems like I don't want to invite her home. Which I don't.

"She works weird hours," I add.

Her face relaxes.

"Is your dad in show biz too?" Maddie asks. She's been quiet till now. Looking for cracks in my story?

"Nope," is all I say.

"What does he do?" Molly asks.

Why are we only talking about my family? "He writes." He calls himself a writer, anyway. "What about your folks?"

"Ugh, they're so boring. A manicurist and a salesperson."

So normal. Lucky.

Nope, can't go there. I have a plan. I'll get out soon.

"What grade are you in?" Maddie asks.

"Twelve."

"Same as us!" Molly says.

"Why did you change schools in your last year?" Maddie demands to know.

"We moved. My school wouldn't let me stay." I could have kept quiet about the move and stayed, but I kind of welcomed the change after a bad couple years with Mom making a spectacle of herself at school events. When she bothered to show up. Which was rarely.

"What did y'all think of the game yesterday?" Maddie says. She fixes a narrow-eyed look at me. I tell myself I should give people the benefit of the doubt, not be so judgy. (A thing kids like me become: hyper-vigilant. Yeah, I've read way too much.)

The others wait for an answer.

Is she talking about a school game? A Toronto team game? What sports are played in the winter? I have no idea.

"Game?" is all I say.

Molly jumps in, talking about some miraculous comeback in

the third quarter. "Leave it to Luca Kitescu," she adds. "That boy is as talented as he is gorgeous."

"I hear he's free," Maddie says. "He finally broke up with Angel. Go get him, girl!"

"I would if I thought he liked athletes, but he likes the influencer wannabes. Oh, speak of the devils."

It's like one of those slo-mo movie scenes. Luca — beefy but muscular, with a Clark Kent vibe, complete with square-framed glasses and the most beautiful jawline I've ever seen — glides across the cafeteria floor and crosses paths with a girl who looks like a goddess and who I assume is Angel the Influencer Wannabe. They look at each other for a split second — time stops, etc. — then continue gliding. Tall, lithe Angel surveys the peasants at the tables she passes with stunning doe eyes. She doesn't look mean either. Even smiles at Molly and Maddie and me as she goes by — the benevolent princess bestowing blessings on her subjects. Then she continues on her way, tossing her glossy brunette mane behind her. Luca sits at a jock table. Beside a guy I can tell from ten yards away is a doofus and whose name, I'm told by Molly, is Will Brown.

Blerg. I have a sad history of doomed crushes. That can't-invite-people-home thing. Plus, who wants to be with a judgy, hyper-vigilant downer?

Anyway, Angel looks like a supermodel at Coachella. There's no way I can compete with that. And I can't get waylaid with distractions this year. Need to get good marks to get out of town.

"Yeah. She's got a ton of Insta followers. Companies are starting to send her free stuff." Molly shows me Angel's IG feed on her phone. Her pix look like pro model shots. "She and Luca were together last year. Before that, there was Anika Jagger, who also has a huge following."

It's a little alarming how much this info crushes me. It isn't like I didn't already know Luca Kitescu was out of my league.

I sneak another glance at the subject of our discussion. She's lowered herself gracefully onto a chair at a table full of other Coachella attendees.

"Must be nice to make money doing nothing," Maddie says, following my glance. I look at her. Maybe her hardness comes from family stuff too.

"Not nothing," Molly says. "She's working it. Don't be a bad feminist. It's okay to like fashion."

"Not working it like we are though — busting our asses doing school, sports, and crappy jobs."

I focus on taking small bites of my tuna sandwich. (What was I thinking, putting in so much filling? So messy!) The conversation switches to the Olympics, and I have absolutely nothing to say about that. And I start to panic because I haven't spoken in so long, but then the conversation turns back to Luca, and Molly turns to me and says, "Luca isn't just a dumb jock. He's super smart. A peer math tutor this year."

"Oh, cool," I say, thankful for something to contribute. "I might just get in touch with him. Algebra's my Achilles' heel." I'm not even lying — it is, and I just might. Haha, I'm definitely a masochist.

"Hey," Molly says a few minutes later as they all jump up to head to basketball practise (*What do I do now?*), "they're still holding tryouts. You should come. You look like you're in shape."

I've always been thin. I've never been in shape. I wasn't planning on getting involved in extracurrics here — cliques are already entrenched, my uni apps are in, and I need a part-time job more than a club to join. But do I want to sit here by myself when they leave? Most emphatically not.

So I head to the gym after stopping at my locker and changing in the bathroom. (Where it sounds like no fewer than three girls are eating their lunches in stalls.)

"Great — you're just in time to run five warm-up laps with the others," says the coach, Ms. Porter, so cheerfully after I introduce myself that I desperately want to please her. She's a wholesome, no-makeup type with great posture.

How hard can it be? Every athlete you hear interviewed goes on about how it's mind over matter, etc. If I just force myself to put one foot in front of the other and make myself keep going at a good pace, I'll do fine. Right?

I'm not sure why I block out the fact that I've always been a phys ed disaster. I'm able to fake it for a couple of laps, and Ms. Porter smiles at me approvingly. I fall a little behind on the third lap and a lot behind on the fourth.

The others look at me while they're running.

And of course, I don't land a single basket when it's my turn at the net because I'm five-foot-two.

"I'm sorry, Kathy," says Ms. Porter crisply when I'm done. "Maybe next year."

Kelsey, I think, but I don't bother to correct her, just nod and hurry into the change room before the others get there.

#BannerDay

2

How's school?

Haha, on a terrible scale of 1-10, an 11

Ugh, sorry

How's Lalaland?

Annoying – a whole city of narcissists
& the other actors' kids r the worst

Ugh, sorry, M

No worries, am taking copious notes – will put them all in a novel one day

Lol, u go, girl, turn those lemons into lemonade!

We just gotta get through the next few months – we will find our people in uni!

From ur lips 2 god's ears, lol

Just imagine … WE'LL NEVER SEE OUR MOMS

CANNOT WAIT

Luv and miss u

SAME

3

MOLLY DOESN'T SEEM TO care about my embarrassing basketball performance. She catches me at my locker after school and invites me to shop with her on Queen Street. "I love your style!" she says. Haha, she has no way of knowing I'm already tired of pretending I'm fashionable. I've also quit trying to improve my selfie game with elaborate app fixes. No point when stunners with movie star names like Angel Aquino exist.

"I could use a personal shopper! You can come to my house for dinner after. Unless your folks expect you home …"

"Nope," is all I say. Just the thought of explaining my situation to her is exhausting. I really should stay away from people this year. I know where this goes. Either they give up on me because I don't invite them home, or when/if I explain, they don't believe how bad it is, given that I look like any other privileged white girl. And I am privileged. I know that. Still sucks.

Even when I explain and they seem to get it, they drop me eventually. Kids like me are pretty much incapable of having fun.

Stupidly, I head with Molly to Le Shop — a new store filled with eco-friendly basics that aren't shapeless sacks for old hippies. This being Parkdale, we pass three guys screaming about the imminent end of the world. Molly doesn't seem fazed, and I guess she's lived here for a while — which tracks, as she isn't of the creative/cool hunter class taking over the area. I guess I fit into that category, but we're here only because my mom's become unhireable, not 'cause we want to be cool.

Le Shop is situated between a cheque cashing place and a liquor store.

"I hate shopping," Molly admits once we're inside. "Pick me out some warm things. Just a few — I'm on a budget."

"Capsule wardrobes are where it's at," I say. I pick out six items for her, and she looks awesome in all of them.

"Omigod, I owe you big time!" she says while cashing out.

"No, you don't," I say. She's so nice. Not a bitter bone in her body. It's just as well this friendship won't get a chance to blossom. I'm not sure I could stand spending loads of time with someone so well-adjusted. (It's official. I'm the worst.)

"Not getting anything?" she asks, sweetly oblivious — even though she lives in Parkdale — to the fact that some of us have zero dollars to spend on clothes. When I shop these days, which is rarely, it's at a no-name thrift shop on Queen. Not the cool kind. Molly doesn't seem the type to root through racks of awfulness.

"Mmm," is all I say. This is going to be a fun game. How many weird responses before Molly gives up on Kelsey?

Bags in hand, we head to her house.

Well, her flat. She and her parents live on the first floor of a TV-type, semi-detached place complete with planters and a welcome mat. It's owned by her uncle, who lives on the second floor, and it's on one of the totally gentrified streets. In contrast, our dilapidated place — on one of the un-gentrified streets — looks like a crack house. Which it kind of is. When the couple we share a wall with aren't shrieking at each other or having extremely loud sex, they're meeting their drug dealer out front. And then, of course, there's my mom on our side.

We're munching on homemade chocolate chip cookies left by Molly's mom with a note about not eating too many before dinner when the chef herself walks in.

"I only ate two!" Molly says, easing in for the hug her mom offers as soon as she throws her jacket on a kitchen chair.

Her mom grins. "As long as you save room for my famous veggie loaf. Gonna whip one up now." She turns bright eyes on me. "And who's this?"

"Kelsey, my mom. Mom, Kelsey."

"So nice to meet you, Kelsey! Call me Leanne."

She's such a … *mom*. Before they get wise to her, people envy me my movie-star-gorgeous mom, but I envy Molly this plump and loving human, off whom kindness rolls in giant waves.

"How was your day?" Leanne asks Molly.

Wow, she actually asks her kid how her day was.

"Good. I met this one." Molly smiles at me.

"Can't have too many friends."

"Don't let her scare you," Molly says to me. "She's missing my brother. At Western."

"Oh, nice," I say politely.

"I do miss your brother, but I would have been friendly to Kelsey, regardless," Leanne says, smiling. "Where do you want to go next year, Kelsey?"

"Oh, I've applied to a few places, but UBC's my top pick."

"So far away!"

The farther the better, I think but don't say, just smile.

Leanne asks me a couple questions about my family and the move that I skillfully dance around, and then she blessedly moves on to informing Molly about the plans for an upcoming family wedding. From the sounds of it, several dozen cousins and aunts and uncles will be jetting into town, and there's a stuffed, multi-day schedule.

Wow, it's like my favorite childhood show, *The Giggle Girls*. The main characters were twins who could always find a sympathetic ear in the form of a beloved auntie, cousin, or grandparent when they were miffed with Mom and Dad. (In contrast, I met one of my ten first cousins, Anya, for the first time at my horrible maternal grandfather's funeral. During the eulogy detailing Gramps' totally invented virtues, Anya leaned over and whispered in my ear, "Think they have the right body?")

Now Molly's asking her mom how *her* day was, and Leanne's sharing a cute anecdote about disappearing lunches in the staff fridge.

"Mom," Molly says when they get off that non-drama, "Kelsey's mom is Hannah Kendler, from *Those Crazy Comics*!"

"Omigosh, Kelsey! We're such fans!"

I paste on a smile.

"I'm going to fangirl so hard when I meet her," Molly says.

Who said you were going to meet her? Yikes. This was a mistake. Now I'm just going to seem horrible when I never invite her home.

"What's she been up to lately?" Leanne asks as she dons an apron (!).

"Taking a bit of a break." A two-year break. Because nobody will hire her.

Leanne nods sagely. "Good to take breaks. Refill the well."

More like refilling her shot glass. And her weed bowl.

"You two feeling okay?" Leanne asks. "So many colds going around."

"We're fine." Molly grins affectionately at Leanne. "You're *such* a mom."

Just then Molly's dad comes through the door booming, "Hey, gang," like we're in a sitcom or something. (Ugh, I'm just hella envious.)

He makes a beeline toward his wife, whom he nuzzles affectionately. "Missed you," he says when he breaks away and throws his jacket on the same chair Leanne did.

"Same," she says, smiling.

"Ahem," says Molly.

"Hey, kiddo." He comes over to give her a hug. "And …"

"This is Kelsey. Kelsey, my dad."

"Nice to meet you, Kelsey. I'm Matt. So, girls, how's school going?"

All the questions. So lovely.

"So far, so good," Molly says. "How 'bout you?"

"Good." Another cute lunchroom anecdote, this one featuring

passive-aggressive notes. "Hey, Kelsey, you like sweet potato fries?" he asks.

"'Course."

He grins. "'Course. I like this girl."

"Dad," says Molly in a lovingly annoyed tone, "everybody likes sweet potato fries. And even if she didn't, she wouldn't tell you when it's obvious you love them so much, right, Kels?"

Eek, I'm "Kels" now. "Probably," I say. "But I really do love them."

"Good. I'm on sides tonight. Sweet potato fries and roasted asparagus. Even if you don't like asparagus, I promise you'll love mine."

"I'm fine with asparagus." I'm fine with anything that doesn't come out of a freezer box. Which most of my meals do.

"Great." With that, he dons a second apron hanging on a hook near the stove and begins to loudly sing the latest Chance the Rapper tune.

"Omigod, Dad, no one wants to hear you rap." Molly looks at me, smiling. "That's our cue to head upstairs."

We go upstairs and scroll through her Insta feed while she gives me the (super sweet and generous) lowdown on people at school.

When I leave, I take a long walk before going home. I need to decompress. It's hard for me to pretend I'm normal for that length of time.

Also, I don't want to go home.

I CAN'T BRING MYSELF to chat with Molly again or eat at the misfit table (don't imagine I'd find somebody else with a narcissistic mother in the entertainment industry to bond with), so the next day, I head outside at lunch. I'm gonna take a long walk to Trinity Bellwoods Park, one hood over, but a no-longer-transitional world away.

Despite the cold weather, there are a few sketchy-looking types congregating at the ditch in front of the school. One of whom catches my eye and raises a hand in a "hi" gesture as I pass, and I'm freaked out for a couple of seconds because, weirdly, he looks like me. Thin, with brown hair and eerily similar facial features. Something passes between us. Not a romantic thing. He feels like the sibling I don't have. The rebel sibling I don't have. A cautionary tale. Not that I'm in any danger of ending up in a ditch. (Am I?)

Ack, I'm desperate for human connection. Definitely imagined that moment.

ONCE AGAIN, MOLLY CATCHES me at my locker at the end of the day.

"Walk with you — give me a minute!"

"Oh, sorry, I'm in a huge rush. I have a … thing."

"Oh, too bad! I was hoping to pop into your house so I could meet your mom."

"Oh. She's … not home."

"Omigod," she says, her eyes widening. "I sound like a stalker, don't I? You're totally afraid of me!"

Better she thinks I'm pulling back 'cause I think she's scary. Which she might be, if she's an actual superfan. A guy once broke into our house, and Mom had to get a restraining order.

"Or maybe you think I'm using you! Omigod, I'm so sorry! What an idiot! I just this minute realized how awful you must think I am! Just for that, I'm not going to mention your mom for … let's say a month! How's that?"

Bad, I think. Then I won't have an excuse for pulling back.

"Great," I say.

"Okay. Again, I'm really, really sorry. I think you're awesome, and I hope we can be friends again."

"No worries," I say.

She gives me a brave little thumbs-up. "I'll make it up to you!" she says, walking away backwards.

"No need," I say. *Just please stop talking.*

"I will!" she calls.

This time, I don't bother answering.

"HEEEEY," MY MOM SAYS, stumbling into the kitchen, where I'm doing my homework.

Yeah, this is why I don't bring people home.

She looks worse every day. She's still ridiculously beautiful — her bod's not even going to pot (haha). But now her eyes and nose are always super red, and there are dark rings under her eyes despite the fact that she spends most of her time sleeping.

Dad's given up hounding her about her drinking and toking. She doesn't think she needs to quit or even cut back.

"Hey," I say back. Why didn't I stay in my room like usual? (I know why. I needed a change of scenery. That'll teach me.) I wait for the questions that never come: How was school? You still feeling sniffly?

Unable to help myself — Molly notwithstanding, I'm a pleaser — I say, "How's your back?" It's been "out" for two years now, since she did a pratfall on *Those Crazy Comics*, that weirdly beloved, offensively named Canadian show featuring has-been comics doing extremely dumb (IMO) physical comedy.

"Lousy," she says, slurring. "Jus' saw the doc. Gave me some stronger pills, finally."

"Good, maybe they'll help," I say.

Or maybe she'll start popping them like Pez too, and then we'll really be up shit's creek.

She shrugs and says, "Going to lie down."

Typical. She has no idea what else to say to me and doesn't realize she should stick around anyway.

Minutes later, Dad comes home from "working" at the library. Pretty early for him — it's dinner time. He's taken to staying away till nine or ten. "What's up?" he says, whipping off his jacket and throwing it down on a broken chair. Everything in this house is broken.

"Not much," I say. Dad asks the questions, but he doesn't necessarily want to hear the answers. Mom takes after her unhinged father, Dad after his distant one. And Mom's issues have made him even more distant — to her, but also to me.

"Where's Mom?" he asks.

The neighbors start screaming, so I wait a few seconds till they stop (one of them storms out) before saying, "Lying down."

"She go to Melnick?"

"Yeah. He gave her new pills."

Just then I hear a noise coming from the cabinet next to the oven. The one we keep all the plastic bags in. It sounds like … something's in there, crinkling the plastic.

"Uh … what's that?" I ask Dad.

He sighs. "Pretty sure it's a rat."

"Excuse me, a what?"

"Saw some droppings last time I opened it. I cleaned it up and put a trap in there."

"Okay, so … do we have an alternate plan?"

Dad doesn't respond, just takes a chicken pot pie out of the freezer and pops it in our ancient oven. The oven door handle falls off, and he jams it back in place, turns the screws, and mutters about how Mom won't even pick up a goddamn screwdriver unless there's vodka in it.

At which moment, the gal who won't even pick up a goddamn screwdriver unless there's vodka in it comes back into the kitchen, muttering, "What's my fault now?"

"Maybe if you bothered to do anything besides lie around and smoke, you'd know."

Three years ago, when I was fourteen, I went through a period of stomping and screaming whenever one of their scenes started. All I ever got from my father was an icy, "This has nothing to do with you, Kelsey." (Does he really believe that or is it what he has to tell himself?) After a while, I gave up on the theatrics, just started quietly leaving when scenes started, vowing to not let any of it affect me.

Hahaha. That's when the sleep paralysis started. Most nights now, just before I fully fall asleep, I feel a threatening presence (or presences) around me and a physical weight on my chest. There are other hallucinations too, and I can't move. Super fun. I've never told my parents about it 'cause there's not much that can be done — I've read up — and they'd probably just brush it off anyway. I've gotten used to the daytime tiredness and figure I'm lucky it only happens once a night. Least I'm not stuck in some horrific *Groundhog Day* situation multiple times every eve. (Small favors, etc.)

By now, I know she'll just walk out in two seconds flat. Sometimes she goes off, but more often, she just takes off, so I don't even bother leaving.

"Back's killin' me," Mom mutters.

"Oh, here we go," says Dad.

"Wassat s'posed to mean? Jesus Christ, Mark!" Her eyes get that hard and glittery look they always get before she goes off, and then she starts in. "Can't even have a minute of peace in my own fuckin' house! Know what? I'm outta here."

Wow, today we're lucky enough to have her go off *and* take off! Coughing. Hopefully it's just destroyed-from-smoking lungs and not the virus we're all hearing about that's spreading like wildfire on the other side of the world.

When she's gone, Dad puts both hands on the counter and says, without turning around to look at me, "Sorry."

He's never said that, and honestly, he doesn't sound all that sorry. I contemplate asking him what he's sorry for. The scene? Their marriage?

I've never been sure why he's stayed. Because he thinks marriage is forever? Because she was — is — his meal ticket?

I decide not to say a reflexive "It's okay," and put my books into my knapsack so I can grab a (cheap, plain cheese) slice at Pizza Pizza and go do my homework at the library.

WHEN I GET HOME, I try to lose myself in winter fashion inspo on IG. But there are only so many jewel-toned cable-knit sweaters a person can look at before getting bored. And I can't afford to buy any of them.

On Twitter, I learn the orange menace to the south of us has started up some drama in the Middle East that'll probably end in a nuclear war. And of course, there are the usual climate change-related disasters and racially-motivated shootings. Just to, you know, add to my ever-present, low-level sense of panic/despair. And everybody's posted pix from the Toronto Women's March. I didn't go 'cause the idea of going alone was just too sad, but now I feel bad. Plus, there's way more info circulating about the deadly virus.

Eek.

I hop back over to Insta, trying to ignore the sound of my mother screaming over the phone at her agent — Dave Green, a super nice guy who tried to get her to rehab and still checks in with her occasionally, even though she's been unhireable for two years. Of course, I have to torture myself by checking out Angel Aquino's feed. Her recent selfies look like stills from a Kendall and Kylie show. I'm not even sure they're photoshopped. They're punctuated by posts — in gorgeous, of-the-moment fonts — saying, "You are loved" and "Life is beautiful."

Ugh.

Despite all my better instincts, I follow Luca Kitescu on Insta, and am gratified when he instantly follows back. Probably because my profile picture's amazing. It was done by a pro photog — a former friend of Mom's. Lucky for me, she didn't friend-dump Mom till after she took my pic. I hope Luca doesn't scroll through my actual feed. There are still a few up there from when I was photoshopping, but the rest are un-touched-up.

Before I can stop myself, I message him about his peer tutoring service. And immediately want to reach into my phone and pull back my message (*Tutoring: where, when, how often?*) once I hit send.

I'm shocked when he answers about ten seconds later ...

Caf, after school, as often as u need it. Get me free while you can. Doing the peer thing for testimonials – gonna start a paid service soon

K, lemme think about it

👍 u new at Queen?

Ya

Where were u be4?

Rosedale Valley

Fancy, why the move?

Better location for my parents

U'll love the hood, it's awesome. Doing anything exciting 2nite?

Oh ya, eating some Ben and Jerry's and watching Happily Ever After (low-rent version of The Bachelor, lol)

V. familiar with HEA, lol, that Courtney's a piece of work

OMG u watch?!

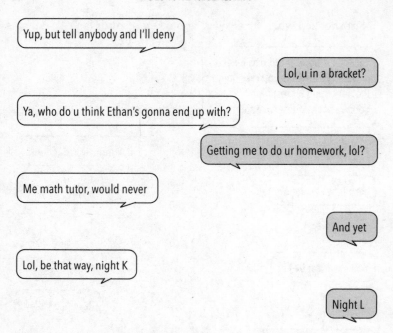

Yup, but tell anybody and I'll deny

Lol, u in a bracket?

Ya, who do u think Ethan's gonna end up with?

Getting me to do ur homework, lol?

Me math tutor, would never

And yet

Lol, be that way, night K

Night L

I go to bed with my heart full (even though I know it won't be enough to ward off the sleep paralysis). Could Mr. Popular have possibly felt the same connection I did just now? It feels impossible, given his superstar status at Queen, but that exchange was such a lovely and unexpected surprise.

I get those so rarely.

4

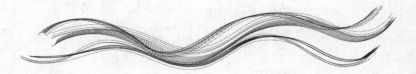

A dozen giant chickens burst out of a pot pie (how did they all fit in there?) and circle my bed, clucking threateningly. I can't move. Can't even scream to chase them away or attract help. Not that my mom would hear. And I wouldn't want my dad to come — he'd just be pissed and say there's no real threat ...

Then rats begin to burst out of the walls and run menacingly toward the chickens, who pivot and start to attack and eat the rats!

Ew, disgusting.

Suddenly Mom's standing over my bed. She doesn't see the chickens or the rats. She senses I'm trying to leave. Wanting to keep me from doing so (not knowing I can't), she sneers, "Where you think you're going?"

Nowhere, I want to scream. I can't move. Can't even talk. Or point to the chickens and rats.

She finally notices them.

She just shrugs. "S'nothin'."

What is wrong with you? I want to scream.

"S'nothin'," she repeats.

Will telepathy work? I focus on sending her my message: Not nothing!

The message doesn't register.

Now Dad's here, saying, "Kelsey, you're being so loud! Keep it down!"

Um, hello, I can't even talk!

He doesn't notice the chickens or rats or even Mom's presence and disappears again.

Wake up, wake up, wake up, I order myself.

And I finally do, but am up a good couple hours before I can finally fall asleep again.

5

"I KNOW YOU COVERED all our health topics in earlier grades but it's important to keep talking about these things. Substance use."

Cue the collective eye roll. It's super unfortunate health classes are taught by gym teachers. Mr. Bolt isn't the worst. He's nice, and he tries. Still, it seems like he's pushing himself to do something he really doesn't want to do. He's like the bad singer at a karaoke party. Painful to watch.

"Shouldn't we talk about the virus?" somebody asks. There've been a couple cases of C-19 confirmed in North America.

"Our public health officials seem on top of it. If anyone experiences the symptoms — a cough and fever, mostly — stay home for the recommended two weeks. Your teachers will keep you up to date. And wash your hands often. Okay, substance use ..."

Pix and stats pop up on the SMART Board, and he has us match dependence levels to substances and guess how long it takes for each substance to metabolize.

This is all punctuated by shouts of, "Yeah!" and "Gotta get me some of that!"

He ignores the heckling. "You may be able to legally purchase some of these substances when you're of age," he says when he's done, "but please be aware that your brain is still developing until the age of twenty-five and all these substances can mess, in varying degrees, with the formation of that all-important white matter. Serious substance use can also result in what? Anybody?"

More jokey responses. "Your ability to get it up?"

"Whether you can get off the couch?"

He ignores all this too and touches the SMART Board once more. "Cognitive impairment, stroke, Alzheimer's disease, and numerous other things. Not to mention the associated risks of smoking anything — emphysema, lung cancer, and so on." Up pops a chart with those stats. "There's also the matter of how serious drug and alcohol use can affect things like motivation and relationships with loved ones. How do you think you would feel if you lived with a substance misuser?"

I doodle a cartoon rat while people throw out comments like, "Would be awesome — my mom wouldn't bug me anymore!"

Bolt winds up with a sigh and, "Any questions?"

I surprise even myself by raising my hand.

Looking equally surprised, he says, "Yes?" (He doesn't know my name yet.)

"OxyContin isn't on that chart," I say. "It should be." It's what Melnick prescribed my mom. I snuck into her room one day while she was in the can to check the label on the new pill bottle. Damn him — doctors aren't even supposed to be prescribing it anymore. Like hello? There's an opioid crisis. But he's an old friend of hers and she can be hella intimidating. Since taking it, she's been even more out of it than usual.

"Yeah, Oxy's the best!" somebody says loudly to laughter.

"You're right," he says, looking at me.

And then the bell rings and Bolt says, "Have a good one, everybody." Everyone leaps up and I get the feeling he's about to ask me something when I pass his desk on the way out, but I pick up speed and make sure I'm out of there before he can.

DITCH GANG GUY FLASHES me a peace sign when I pass him outside at day's end. We've progressed beyond the generic half wave. Is he a little thinner than he was a couple days ago? Maybe I'll actually talk to him sometime. I haven't managed to make any other friends since meeting Molly and Maddie. Not even the glommers I usually attract. Sadly, this dude's my closest one.

GIVEN MY FAMILY'S NEW(ISH) financially-strapped status, it's on me to pay for college. Which means that, in addition to nabbing a scholarship — or two or three — I need a part-time job other than babysitting. Which will have the added benefit of keeping me away from home a good part of the time and maybe even help me find some friends who won't want to meet my mom.

I soon land a gig in the hood, at an about-to-open dipped soft serve place called Soft Spot. I've always had a passion for dipped soft serve, but I think it's extremely weird that an ice cream place is opening in the middle of a Canadian winter. Also, the flavors,

dips, and toppings are kind of ho-hum compared to the wild —
often wildly awful — flaves featured in the million other new
ice cream shops on Queen. And I'm not sure soft, lounge-type
furniture — get it? — and ice cream is a good combo. I'm pretty
sure the enterprise is doomed to fail, and quickly. But beggars
can't be choosers.

At a training session before opening day, I find out the
owner is a sweet, older-but-just-starting-her-life-in-business woman.
(Which answers my question, who thought this was a good
idea?) She says to the first couple of us to arrive, "Hello, I'm Ruth.
Let's wait for the others to arrive before we start — there are six
of you altogether."

"Hey, do I know you?" asks the guy next to me a couple seconds
later.

It isn't asked in a slimy way. He looks as awkward as I feel,
and I'm pretty sure he's just trying to be friendly. I'm grateful I
no longer have to fake a Very Important Text Conversation.

"Don't think so. Kelsey. Kendler." There I go again, tossing out
my last name because I can't think of anything else to say.

"Lee Lang."

"We should start an alliterative name club."

He gives me a quick "Ha," then launches into a monologue
about how he doesn't expect to work here long; he's started doing
television and movie reviews complete with dramatic re-enactments on TikTok.

"Cool," I say politely when he pauses for air. Then I introduce
myself to the quiet girl hunched in the corner next to me. "Hi,
I'm Kelsey."

"Hi," she says (quietly). "I'm Ruby."

A girl who looks like the total opposite of Ruby, personality-wise, swishes up to us and, after an appraising glance, says, "Hi, introverts huddling in the corner. I'm Quinn."

I say hi, even though she was rude (albeit correct). Then it's her turn to launch into a monologue similar to Lee's about how this is just a temporary situation for her; she's actually an actress who just graduated from one-liners on TV shows to larger parts, and it's pretty exciting.

When I — pathetically — googled "How to make friends" the morning of my first day at Queen, I found an article by a psychologist that said most people aren't as focused on you as you think: they're mostly consumed by their own lives. I didn't believe her, but now I think she may have been onto something.

Lee asks Quinn if she'd be interested in appearing in one of his TikTok movie re-enactments, and she just laughs and shows him her own TikTok profile. She has ten thousand followers.

Two other kids come in, and when Quinn finally takes a break from Monologue Number Two — this one about her family, apparently full of similarly outsized personalities — one of them says, "Hi, everybody, I'm Chelsea."

"I'm Veer," the other one says.

Chelsea is a tiny, chirpy redhead wearing cat eye glasses, a pink pullover with a Peter Pan collar, and a fifties-style skirt with poodles all over it. I'm guessing she's also a drama kid, though not of the same stripe as Quinn — more aspiring stage actress than future Disney star. Veer is her quiet foil.

"Hi," I say. "I'm Kelsey." Quinn and Ruby and Lee introduce themselves.

"Looks like we're all here," I say. "Ruth said there were six of us." Aw, listen to me, making small talk.

Chelsea looks at me and says, "You have such a nice energy. Doesn't she, Veer?"

Veer says, "Yup." I sense he has a few canned, one-word responses for talkative Chelsea. Whose comment about my nice energy has me feeling ridiculously touched.

On cue, Ruth walks over to us and says, "Okay, hello everyone." Then she proceeds to train us on the soft serve machine, experiencing an alarming number of problems. "It's actually very easy," she says (lies?) when it finally works. "You'll figure it out. You all start tomorrow. Opening day. Come at ten forty-five. The store opens at eleven. I've just opened another location in North York, and I'll be there. My niece will be managing this store — Kira."

Who shows up stoned the next weirdly warm (Saturday) morning, when there's a lineup halfway down the block.

"Wow," says Kira, staring, red-eyed. Manager material, this girl is not.

We're all dressed in the Soft Spot sweatshirts and visors Ruth gave us, and I quickly realize it's up to me to take charge. I order Chelsea, who goes to a performing arts school (I was right about her), to sing songs with the people waiting to get in, along with Quinn. Once the doors open, they'll double as greeters. Inside, I figure out an assembly-line type of system. I put Lee, Veer, and Ruby at the topping stations, and a still stunned-looking Kira on cash. She'll be slow, but she's the only one who knows how to use the register 'cause she's worked at the North York store. I'll work the soft serve machine. *Just one machine for all those people? Don't think about it ...*

I take a few minutes to figure out how to use the thing — Ruth's training was decidedly sub-par — and I have a minute of panic when it jams. Hoping that rebooting it like a computer will help, I shut it off, clean it out, start it again, and to my everlasting relief, it works.

"Yeah, you have to do that every now and then," says Kira, after the fact.

I open the door and ... stampede.

Chaos reigns for the next nine hours. I give everybody except me a short break, scarfing down some soft serve during one brief lull.

I really hope this job doesn't get me hating soft serve.

Ruth shows up at closing time and is happy with the sales figures.

"Now chop candy for tomorrow's toppings in the basement kitchen," she orders us, adding, "and clean up. The machines and counters, but also the slipcovers. There's an industrial strength washing machine and dryer in the basement and stain remover." Oh god, I'll have to wait for the slipcovers to be clean and dry and put them back on the loungers before going home ...

After glaring at Kira, who took several weed breaks over the course of the day and whose eyes are as red as stop signs now, Ruth gives me the key and her suppliers' phone numbers and tells me to call when I'm low on things, adding, "I can see I can't rely on Kira. I'll give you a twenty-five cent raise."

Yee-haw.

I'm exhausted even before I start chopping candy for toppings and wrestling the tightly fitted slipcovers off the loungers.

"She died as she lived," I mutter to myself as I fight with the slipcovers, "doing stupid shit all by herself."

6

NEWS

??

A MAN AND A JOB

Yay! Do tell!

Peer math tutor

Beginning of a porno, lol

Lolllllllll

Job?

New ice cream place

Opening in the winter?

I know, doomed, right?

Lol, just gotta get u through summer till uni

Ya! Hope it lasts that long!

Nice people?

Maybe – can't tell yet

The guy?

Cute. Started up a text convo

Almost married, lol

Haha, gives me hope.

Suggest reading books instead

Lol, r things better over there?

Nope

Aw, sorry.

Happy things r looking up for u tho!

Wouldn't go that far, lol

Lol, we're too young to be this misanthropic

Ha, glad I have u 2 b misanthropic with 🖤

Same! 🖤

7

FAMILY DAY, THAT RENOWNED (not) Canadian hol, is fast approaching.

Everyone at work's super enthused for the long weekend. Ruby's looking forward to board game competitions with her parents; Lee, to a Miyazaki festival with his friends; Veer, to heading up north with his fam; and Quinn, to visiting film biz ('course) relatives in Vancouver. Chelsea, naturally, is the most extra person ever about holidays, even fake ones, and rhapsodizes about all her family's traditions, which include winter hikes and hand-knit sweaters for everybody. Even Ruth is super excited. Winter flavors have infected the entire menu. (Better late than never.)

"Wait till you taste the Marvelous Maple!" Chelsea enthuses.

"Lol, maple was the best Ruth could do?"

"Ha." She gives me a puzzled look, and I feel like the Grinch.

"Kidding! Pretty sure I need the full Marvelous Maple experience!"

Her smile returns. "You really do!" She sighs happily. "I just love holidays, don't you?"

I don't. (Also, this isn't a real holiday.) "I do!"

Now Veer's the one to give me an odd look as he slips me a taster.

I try my best to smile.

JUST BEFORE OUR FAMILY Day meal — a ritual that's stuck even though we haven't been a happy family (or eaten together) for ages — I listen to a popular motivational podcast called *You're Amazing!* The host, Dr. Ashley (yeah, hard to take her seriously), has an Insta account featuring a lot of pithy sayings against rose-gold backdrops, à la Angel. Also many photos of her gorgeous thirty-something self, her Insta-perfect husband and her two beautiful kids standing by windows with spectacular views.

Okay, I know, but my New Start's off to an extremely rocky beginning, and I need all the help I can get.

"I'd like to wish my listeners a very happy Family Day," Dr. Ashley says in her velvety voice. "Family Day is the perfect time to cultivate gratitude. Here are some mantras I chant on holidays. I am grateful to be alive and healthy — and by the way, let's all stay healthy by washing our hands often. I am grateful to have family and loved ones with whom to share the holiday. I will face bad behavior with grace. I will enjoy the holiday."

I silently repeat the mantras as I force-march myself to the dining room, where the sound of scuffling rats (and the neighbors' sex play) isn't quite as loud as it is in the kitchen.

I am grateful to be alive and healthy.

And that Mom is coughing probably because she has smoker's lung and not the virus ...

Our dinner table conversation is no different than the usual.

My dad fixes an accusing look at my mom and says, "The wildlife guy says rats reproduce like crazy, and he saw more than one in the cabinet and thinks the little ones have gotten into the walls — there are wall noises in the kitchen."

"They're not in the goddamn walls," Mom slurs in a raspier-than-usual voice. Shit, she better not have the virus. She's totally wasted. Her eyes are bright red. She also stinks, her pajamas are stained, and the top's done up wrong. "He wants our money, s'all!"

"Omigod, you are unbelievable!"

"Happy Family Day," she mutters. She tries to lift a wine glass, but drops it instead. It shatters, and red wine spreads in a bloody puddle all over the valuable but ragged Persian rug under the dining room table.

I am grateful to have family and loved ones with whom to share the holiday meal.

"Dammit, Hannah," Dad yells, bouncing out of his seat to get some club soda from the fridge.

"Doneed this. Feel like shit," she mutters and gets up, bumping into the wall before she rights herself and weaves down the hallway to her room, coughing.

I will face bad behavior with grace.

Dad and I proceed to eat in silence.

"How's the writing going?" I ask finally. Why do I always have to be the grown-up?

"Okay," he mutters. "School good?"

His phrasing and tone indicate he just wants a confirmation, so I say, "It's okay," hoping, as I always do, that he'll pick up on something in my own tone and realize it is, in fact, extremely not okay. But of course he doesn't, just finishes his meal quickly and says he's going outside for a minute. (He smokes too — cigarettes and the occasional joint. But makes a very big point — especially when Mom's around — of smoking outside.)

How did I get stuck with these two?

When I excuse myself to go to the bathroom, I bump into Mom — dammit — going in.

"Feeling bad, huh?" Why do I always feel I have to say something? When will I give up the stupid hope that this time, she too will act differently — tell me she's sorry and that she loves me? (Not that I love her. Do I? How can I, even if I want to?)

She mutters something incomprehensible.

"Maybe see a surgeon?" Why can't I just stop talking?

"Soft tissue, no operation," she mumbles.

"It's just … all the booze and weed and pills …" Now, why did I say that?

She rolls her eyes. Yup, that was a big mistake. "Like father, like daughter."

"I'm just worried about you," I say, my stomach churning. Did she actually just diss me?

She closes her eyes and says, "Kelsey, I'm in a lotta fuckin' pain here."

"I know!"

"Just lemme alone ..."

With that, she shuffles into the can. (Coughing. And not into her elbow.)

Right. What did she ever do to deserve a daughter who was so selfish as to express concern about her? And who's sacrificed a social life of her own to keep her secrets.

And who wants to not catch the virus.

When I'm back at the table and Dad's finished blotting the wine stain with club soda — which doesn't do very much — he sits back down and he and I gobble down our chicken pot pie (yep, again) in record time and near silence. Then, over cherry pie, he decides to jabber away about some coffee shop drama involving a mixed-up order, pretending this is all fine — that Mom didn't just throw a fit over nothing and that we aren't our own weird, lonely island of two.

I will enjoy the holiday.

The fake normalcy can last only so long. Mom wanders back into the dining room and looks at us with unseeing eyes. There's something new this time. She looks like she doesn't even know where she is.

She puts a hand to her head and says, "Diz ..." She starts to fall. Dad leaps up and catches her by the arm on one side. I jump up too, to catch her on her other side. She straightens slightly and mumbles, "Can do misself."

"Jesus," Dad mutters. He puts his arm around her shoulder, and I try to do the same with her other arm, but she fights me.

"S'okay," she mutters.

It's not. Her face is white and sweaty, and her skin is cold and clammy. I keep trying to grab her arms, but she continues to flail around.

Until she stops both talking and fighting, and suddenly, she's nearly dead weight.

Now I'm able to put her arm around my shoulder. She's heavy as hell. I feel a stabbing pain in my own lower back.

"Dad, maybe we should call an ambu—"

"She's conscious. She's fine. We just have to walk her around, keep her awake."

We do that, walking her in a circle from the kitchen to the living room and back to the kitchen again. I nearly let go at one point.

"Don't let go," Dad says sternly.

Mom mumbles, "Where you takin' me?"

"I really think we should call an ambulance," I say.

"She'll be fine," says my dad, feeling her pulse.

I wonder how he knows, since we've never seen her this way.

"You gonna pretend this isn't bad too?" I ask.

He ignores that.

After a while, Dad seems to think it's okay to take her to bed. Don't know how he knows, as he never went to medical school.

Once we get her to her room and into bed, her eyes close instantly, and I tell Dad she's been taking way more Oxy than she's supposed to (the bottle's almost empty and shouldn't be, given when the prescription was filled), and also, she's not supposed to drink while taking it, which clearly she's been doing.

Dad shakes his head and says, "I know she wouldn't overdo the Oxy."

Then why the hell do you think she's acting the way she is? I point at the bottle. "Count the pills."

This gives him pause, but then he says, "Kelsey, you're over-reacting."

Omigod. He's still in denial. Why?

Never mind, I know the answer to that too.

His life's in way worse shape than he thought.

"Dad, we need to talk to her. Enough's enough."

"As long as you remember it's the drugs talking," he surprises me by saying after a second.

That and the terrible personality, I think. In the highly unlikely case I ever became dependent on substances, I'm pretty sure I'd at least have some awareness of how my altered state would affect the people around me. Why doesn't she have that?

Mom opens her eyes and mutters, "Y'all shit talking me?"

Dad looks at me for a second like he thinks maybe this wasn't a good idea after all.

I'm thinking the same thing.

Doesn't she realize normal mothers don't talk to their kids this way? What am I supposed to say?

I decide on, "We're worried about you." Too late, I remember how she reacted the last time I told her I was worried about her.

She laughs shortly and says, "Yeah, right."

Okay, now I'm pissed. "What's that supposed to mean?" My heart's beating a mile a minute.

"Nags," she mutters.

"Excuse me?"

"Kelsey," Dad warns.

She looks at me and says, "You have no idea what it feels like to be me. To live my shitty life."

In my head, I'm screaming a whole monologue (am too afraid

of her to do it out loud): *Nags? We're nags? For wanting you to get off drugs? I think you have it backwards, lady. Try appreciating what you have, why don't you?*

I'm dimly aware I should follow that last bit of advice myself, but at the moment, I'm too full of self-pity. Needless to say, I don't utter any of this, just run to my room.

Their yelling goes on for a good half hour.

She's not normal, he's not normal — nothing about our life is normal.

I don't expect my life to change significantly at college — in fact, I'm highly doubtful it will. But a girl can hope.

I also hope I can hang on till then.

IN MY ROOM, I don't go on social media. I have zero desire to see pix of everybody else's merrymaking. Especially Angel Aquino's.

But later that night, Molly texts me a photo. *Hope you're having a fab weekend! Here's us!*

This only serves to remind me she'd never get that there's no chance of having a "fab" weekend at my house.

The next message is from … Luca!

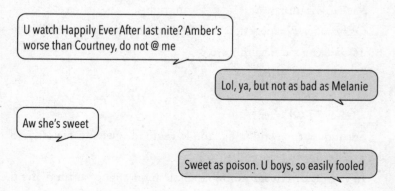

U watch Happily Ever After last nite? Amber's worse than Courtney, do not @ me

Lol, ya, but not as bad as Melanie

Aw she's sweet

Sweet as poison. U boys, so easily fooled

I think ur sweet – u fooling me?

Aw TX, but maybe, ya

Don't believe that

Don't u think everybody has good and bad in them?

Ya for sure but one always comes out ahead and ur defs more good than bad

How would u know?

Good instincts about ppl, tho I've been wrong

Want to know more about the wrongs, but don't want 2 b nosy

See? Ur good

It's official, I think when I sign off after he tells me to have awesome dreams. Luca Kitescu can never know the dark, mean thoughts I have. He wouldn't get me. Just like Molly.

I'm sure he isn't thinking about me as a potential girlfriend. He's never suggested we meet. And we don't have any classes together. I should probably just end our text relationship. If I didn't answer even one time, he'd probably never text again. Guys like Luca don't need girls like me.

Maybe that's why I feel okay continuing our textlationship. It isn't real. There's no danger of him wanting to meet my mom.

And he's saying nice things about me. Even though he doesn't know me.

If he did, he probably wouldn't.

8

Mom's holding a carving knife over me. I can't move.

She hands me a goblet of blood. "Drink," she orders me.

I try to croak a "No," but I can't.

Then, Doc Ashley's on the other side of my bed, holding out a goblet, saying, "No, she needs to drink this!"

I want to tell her people shouldn't drink essential oils, but I can't.

Then Luca joins the party and says, "Who are they?"

I want to tell him something, but don't know what to say.

He shakes his head and walks away.

I want to beg him to come back, but I can't.

"Drink!" screams Mom.

"Drink!" screams Doc Ashley.

Dad comes in, annoyed. "What's going on?"

I want to tell him they're trying to get me to drink stuff I shouldn't drink, but I can't.

"Kelsey, what's wrong with you? Just drink it!"

I want to tell him why I shouldn't, but I can't.

He shakes his head. "Always making trouble."

Me? I want to screech incredulously. But I can't.

"Just ignore them!" he says.

Does he see the knife? The blood?

How can I ignore them?

Mom moves her goblet to my lips.

Doc Ashley moves hers to my lips.

Drink, drink, drink, they chant.

Wake up, wake up, wake up …

And I finally do, wondering if I'll ever get a decent night's sleep again …

9

I DON'T REMEMBER MY parents fighting as much when I was really young. I think for a long time my dad tried just not responding to Mom's complaints and insults. He'd probably never even heard his (cool, aloof) parents argue.

We almost never did things like family trips. Once Mom started making some decent coin, they took yearly vacations without me. If they were speaking. They could go months at a time just grunting at each other once Dad decided to stand up for himself during arguments and not just let things pass.

But I do remember that sometimes, when I was really little — like, kindergarten-aged little — she would let me come curl up beside her on the couch when she was lying down. (Which, even then, was often.) If someone asked me for one nice memory of my mom, that would probably be it. Even though it doesn't involve her doing or saying anything remotely affectionate.

There are way more bad memories than good. Like the time she made me miss my ballet recital 'cause she got into a drunken skirmish just before we were supposed to leave, and Dad had to clean her up.

And the first time she totaled a car, about six months after recital night. She totaled another one about a year after that. And a third one a year after that.

At that point, I refused to get in the car with her driving.

"Whaddya mean, no? Get in the car," she said when she came to pick me up at a classmate's house one night. I'd told Dad I wouldn't drive with her anymore, even if she was sober. Even when not under the influence, she was careless and distracted and got super aggressive if called out by other drivers, increasing the chances of an incident. But I guess he thought I was bluffing.

"I don't feel safe in the car with you," I told her, my stomach churning. I cursed myself for not having made another plan from the beginning. "I'll walk or call a cab. Or get a lift with someone else."

"Goddammit, Kelsey, get in the car," she shouted when, ugh, there were a bunch of people on the porch. It was my first (would be my only) seventh grade party.

I saw the porch people jab elbows.

"Please stop shouting," I begged Mom.

"Then get in the car," she shouted.

I started walking, my heart hardening further. It was fall and not too cold or too dark. It was only about a half hour walk to my house.

Finally, she shouted, "Well, fuck you too," and raced away.

I kept walking and forced myself not to look back.

Nobody came after me.

At home, Dad asked me where she was. I reminded him I'd told him I wouldn't drive with her, and his response was, "Goddammit, Kelsey!"

I knew what he was thinking. She was probably headed to some bar to get wasted and there was a good chance she'd total another car on the way home — possibly her own. Again.

And it would be my fault.

Sure enough, she came home around two in the morning, blasted, but in one piece. (I swear, she has nine lives.)

She rarely spoke to me directly after that, but it wasn't like she'd ever spoken to me much anyway. She'd come home from work, rant and rave about how someone she worked with had it in for her, and flop out on the couch, in front of the TV, with a bottle. No greeting, no questions, nothing. For me or for Dad.

The worst memories are of parties. She was the same at them as she was on stage. Used the same cruel, crude language. Which, in the early part of her career got her marked as cool and subversive. But even in the comedy world, that stuff gets old fast. Just comes off as bitter and angry at a certain point.

One night when I was about thirteen, we were at a neighbor's barbecue when the topic turned to movie stars, and Mom said about some new heartthrob, "Yeah, that one's got all the ladies creaming in their pants."

I was standing about two feet away from her with a group of neighborhood kids. Whose parents, standing around my mom, looked horrified.

I'd been on edge for the first twenty minutes or so of the party, but then had relaxed. (Silly me.) I'd even even been doing well socially, contributing to a lively exchange about high-rise jeans vs. low risers.

Dad turned beet red.

Mom, of course, didn't even register the reactions.

Conversation started up again in their group after a couple seconds, and I realized people kept rushing into the conversation so Mom wouldn't talk again. Before this, they'd let her hold court. When they were still delighted to have a semi-celeb in their midst. Now, a half hour in, they had her number.

The people in my circle did what they always did when something like this happened. They stopped looking at me. Sometimes in this situation, somebody would say something like, "Wow, your mom, huh?" in a way that meant, "Wow, your mom's super embarrassing, huh?" But that didn't happen this time.

A few minutes later, when my crowd had completely deserted me and I'd moved closer to Mom and Dad, Dad spilled pop all over his T-shirt and mine and Mom's. I had to admire the instantly improvised can choreography that trick required. He apologized profusely to our hosts and said we'd be back after we changed.

Yeah, right.

It was around then she stopped thinking she should have to audition for stuff. Even still, she managed to nab a role as a sarcastic political advisor in a movie featuring several Hollywood heavyweights. We all thought it was going to be her big break.

Until the night she came home ranting and raving about how they were all dumb as shit, blah, blah, blah.

She never went back to set and there was no more talk in our house about that movie. Especially when it won seven academy awards — one of which went to the actress in the role that had once been hers.

Dad tried, at one point, to get her to go to AA meetings. Naturally, she wouldn't. But he did — surprisingly — take me to an Al-Anon meeting, for families of alcoholics, when I was fourteen. It was a kind of admission that something was wrong, and we'd been affected. Though I would have appreciated a verbal acknowledgment of this on his part, this was the next best thing, and I was touched.

People were friendly (a little too) when we came in. After some mingling, we were called to sit down. The meeting's chair recited what seemed like a standard opening spiel, telling us that Al-Anon was a safe, anonymous space offering support to those living with serious drinkers. But after the opening statement, she lost me a bit, listing the twelve steps — the same twelve steps the alkies follow. Apparently, we were supposed to follow them too.

There's an awful lot about god in those steps, and needless to say, I'm not a believer. It's too hard to buy that somebody's watching out for me, and if somebody is, they're doing a shit job.

Next, the woman talked about the big principle of Al-Anon — detaching with love. We were charged to "encourage and support" our addicts — but also take care of ourselves first. This seemed to me like speaking out of both sides of one's mouth. And how did one support an addict, anyway?

Some meetings were sharing meetings and others featured topics and speakers. This was a sharing meeting. The first person to get up and share a story was a sixty-something man who said after thirty years of marriage, he was still trying hard to support his wife and detach with love, and he kept tripping up, but he was certain one day god would show him the way. My dad's eyes dulled a bit at "thirty years of marriage," and even more after "god." (Dad's not a believer either. Probably for the same reason I'm not.)

Another sharer with a similar story got up next, and then came a twenty-something girl I'd looked forward to hearing. But once she started talking, it became evident she was kind of a disaster, and I wasn't really interested in that glimpse into my possible future so I tuned her out and instead, studied the schedule of upcoming meetings.

Some of the topics seemed interesting. Dealing with Anger was one. "Are you told to control your anger when others are allowed to violently explode?" Why, yes. "Do you feel empty and fill the void with unhealthy substitutes for love?" Back then, I didn't have any experience with unhealthy relationships, but I sure knew about junk food.

Unfortunately, many other topics turned me off. Under the topic of Control, for example, we were ordered to "Let go and let God!" Eek, the god thing again.

As far as I was concerned, we all needed psychologists more than this never-actually-proven-effective organization. But we didn't have the dough. Also, I suspected Dad didn't want to face the fact that he'd made some pretty bad life decisions.

The only help Al-Anon gave me came in the form of a book list. It was then I read everything I could about children of people with substance issues and realized I had many of the common traits. I also learned that kids like me were, rather mystifyingly, at increased risk of becoming addicts ourselves.

At least that fate, I was quite certain, would never befall me.

10

U see what's happening in Italy?

Ya, hard to take in

Everybody on my mom's set is sick, but she says it's colds

Winter colds in L.A.?

Lol, to them it's freezing!

Wimps, lol

Hope it doesn't spread here!

Already a few confirmed cases. Hopefully they can contain it

Scary

Ya, but public health depts r on it

Ur better off there – here, the orange guy's just hoping it'll magically disappear. We're doomed. Fingers crossed for u there tho! How goes it otherwise?

It goes

How much free ice cream u eating, lol

Boring flavors, lol. How're things with the mom?

Terrible. Constantly on my case to socialize with the horribles, lol

Ugh, sorry

On ur end?

She's retired entirely from parenting. Holes up in her room. Drinking and drugging much worse

Ugh, so sorry

I know u r 🖤

The man?

Still texting

Just texting? Lol, don't u go to the same school?

Ya, weird, I know, but also nice? (Also, u don't much like the phone or in-person get-togethers, lol. Maybe he same?)

Ha, true. Have perfected the introvert life. But with guys, could be something else. Be careful

Can't b any more careful, lol. Most careful girl in world

Ugh, side effect of living with wild ones

Uh-huh

Take it easy. Don't catch cold, lol

Lol, u 2. Love u 🖤

Luv u too 🖤

11

I'M NOT SURE HOW I'm going to juggle my Soft Spot shifts —
I'm booked to work twenty hours a week — and my mountains
of homework. I wonder how dynamos like Molly, who landed a
job at Le Shop and does a million extracurrics too (all the sports,
plus she's yearbook editor), do it. Possibly, the key is coming from
families that don't exhaust them.

But I'm thinking Ruth's being insanely optimistic. After opening day, we went back to seasonal temps, and the crowds died
right down. Hopefully the place will still be busy enough to give
me a reasonable number of shifts, but not enough to kill me.

"Hey," I say to Ruby and Lee when I get there one day, and
they tell me Quinn's due in too, but not Veer or Chelsea. Okay,

good. That means Ruth has, in fact, realized she has to scale down at least a little.

"Hey," Ruby says in a voice barely above a whisper.

I thought *I* was quiet before I met Ruby Mills.

While we're prepping, Lee asks me if I've watched that old show *The Wire*, and I say no. He tells me I really should, and I tell him it's highly unlikely I ever will.

Then Quinn comes in, looks at us and shakes her head. "What a group."

"Hello to you too," I say.

She looks at me and shrugs. "Don't mind me. I hate everything and everybody." She shoves her jacket onto the shelf under the counter. "I may have sociopathic tendencies." She looks like she's about to say something else — an explanation of some kind? That girl's got walls thick as tree trunks around her, and I suspect she has a story. But then she clamps her mouth shut, and the jaded look takes over again.

"Hopefully, you'll tamp down those tendencies while you're here," I say to fill the silence.

She rolls her eyes and says, "I see you."

Okay, I have to laugh.

"So what do you do, hobby-wise?" she asks me as we uncover the topping trays. "Aside from photoshopping Insta pix?"

"Ouch," I say.

"Too on the nose?"

"I don't do that anymore."

"Glad to hear it. You don't need to."

"Aw, thanks."

"I meant the photoshopping doesn't help so it's not worth your time."

"Ha, okay. Right."

"I mean, unless you're Angel Aquino, who's already gorge and who Photoshop turns into a goddess." Quinn doesn't even go to our school, but Angel's a local celebrity. She whips her phone out of her jeans pocket and punches up her Insta feed. "Never a step wrong, amirite?"

I look at Angel skating on a frozen pond, arms outstretched, her perfect face turned up to the bluer-than-blue sky.

"When you're right, you're right."

"Your profile pic's good though. Was it taken by Daria Good?"

"It was," I say.

"Thought so. She's great. Did my headshots."

At the mention of "headshots," Ruby looks mega intimidated.

To put her at ease (and to keep Quinn from asking what Daria Good was doing taking my picture), I decide to change the subject. "So I hope people keep coming. And that the crazy virus doesn't get worse here." I realize belatedly this new topic will do just the opposite of putting Ruby at ease. I decide to tell a dumb joke. "Why is it called the novel coronavirus?"

Quinn rolls her eyes. "Why?"

"It's a long story."

Ruby laughs, and Quinn glances at her. "Omigod, she can laugh. Do you speak too?"

She smiles slightly. "I can, yes."

"Well, who would have thought you're a secret chatterbox? Now that I know you can speak, care to share anything? Caveat emptor. I may respond in a way that makes you regret confiding in me."

Poor Ruby is saved when I open the door to a couple of waiting customers.

AS IF I'M NOT suddenly busy and overwhelmed enough (#Be CarefulWhatYouWishFor), I decide to sign up for driving lessons to keep me away from home even more. I know before I even start that it's a terrible idea. Thanks to Mom, I already know I'll be a nervous driver, especially in snowy, icy weather. And I'm not exactly thrilled to be stuffed into a tin can with a bunch of other people, given the virus.

I tell myself I didn't have much choice about driving. I'd feel like even more of a failure/freak if I didn't take lessons and get my license like everybody else. (With the possible exception of Ditch Gang Guy, who's still braving the outdoors, even as his freezing ditch mates have abandoned him. He looks cold and shivery whenever I see him, and I wonder why he doesn't just go inside. Is he even enrolled at Queen?)

My lesson mates are Will Brown and Angel Aquino's bestie, a chronic giggler named Maya. Thank the universe Luca's not in my group. That's the only silver lining of this situation.

As if I'm not nervous enough, Will provides a running commentary while I'm driving, with Maya giggling at his every word.

"Holy shit, Kelsey," he shrieks when I'm back in the parking lot, having been swiftly exiled from the street by our instructor, "he said roll to a stop! Everybody check your necks!"

"That's enough now," says our instructor, Alan, with absolutely no authority in his tone.

DESPITE THE INCREASING NUMBER of virus cases, the total disaster that is driving school, and talk of an impending teacher strike (which I cannot let myself think about because that would mean being stuck at home with you-know-who), I'm feeling pretty good, thanks to continuing text exchanges with Luca, Molly finally backing off on meeting my mom, and a nice work rhythm with Chelsea, Veer, Lee, Ruby and Quinn. And Kira, who's smoking a little less and seems grateful I'm running the place. My work friends will never be real friends — I can't invite them home, and none of them have made any moves to invite me anywhere — but it's nice to spend time with them at the shop. And we group text occasionally, mostly when people need to switch shifts, but also sometimes just for fun. Chelsea's big on asking stuff like, Are you a dog person or a cat person? (In answer to that one, Veer texted "Dragon" with a wink emoji.)

And then.

One day, Molly meets me after my shift and insists on walking home with me.

A month has passed. I have no out.

I know it's going to end badly before we even start walking.

Sure enough, when we reach my house, I see my mom on the front walk, looking like she has no idea how she got there and also like she doesn't care. She's giggling and muttering to herself.

High as a kite.

"K, see you tomorrow," I say to Molly, not even caring that I sound rude, desperately hoping she'll just say, "Oh, okay, bye."

But of course, she doesn't. "Is this your house?" she says. "Do you know her?" She gestures to my mom. "We used to have bad neighbors too. They mostly just yelled, though. Druggies are the worst."

"Yeah, I'll just go past her quickly. See you!"

"I'll go with you," she says before I take off. "She's probably harmless, but I've never seen her before, and she might be dangerous. She's less likely to do something if there are two of us."

"But then you'll have to go by her alone when you head out," I say, my mind working furiously.

"I'll stay for a while."

Shit.

I'm trying to think of a response when Mom seems to register our — my — presence and starts to walk (stumble) over to us.

Double shit.

But wait. Molly doesn't realize it's my mom. She remembers the Hannah Kendler of old. Since the Oxy, Mom's standards have dropped even further, and Molly has no idea this person with unbleached, uncombed hair, no makeup and stained clothes is her former idol. I silently hope Mom won't let the cat out of the bag.

"You can't stay," I say. "I have to go out again. I have a … thing." I vaguely recall saying this to her another time and once again, I hate myself for being so rude. (Even though I'm kind of frustrated with her for continuing to push. Of course I'm mostly frustrated with my mom, who's the cause of my rudeness.) "I'll just quickly go by her, grab what I need and leave again."

"I'll wait here for you."

"I don't want to leave you with her," I say again.

"Okay, I'll go in with you," she says. I sense her mounting frustration. She wanted to come inside with me in the first place.

Mom's suddenly right beside us.

Shit, shit, shit.

And that's when she ruins everything. "Hey, you're my kid," she says, giggling.

I can't bring myself to say, "No I'm not." I can't go that far.

It was all bound to come crashing down anyway.

I see the light slowly dawning on Molly's face.

I feel myself go red. I feel sick.

Not only has my mom revealed herself as the weird, strung-out lady, I've been revealed as an unstable liar myself.

I hate her so much for putting me in this position. I know serious substance use comes from pain, but how does she not see that she's doing to me what she once told me her unhinged dad did to her? (I also know she may have a mental illness and be self-medicating — she isn't *like* other parents. So why doesn't she get help? Especially now that we live a stone's throw away from the country's best addiction and mental health facility?)

Molly looks at me. "This is …"

"Yeah," I mutter.

"Who are you?" Mom demands, poking a finger in Molly's face. "You're not my kid." She giggles. "But maybe you are. Ooh, I'm feeling good."

I have no idea what to say, what to do.

"You're pretty," she says to Molly. "Give her some tips," she adds, gesturing in my direction and cackling.

I want to die.

But I have to think of something to say first.

Before I can say anything, Molly says to me in a low voice, "Is there a way we can get her inside?"

And I think for a wild second that maybe this will turn out okay after all. That Molly will help me deal with Mom and hang with me for a while after, during which time she'll tell me she has a relative with an alcohol or drug problem too, and that I can always count on her — that I can call or text anytime, come over whenever I need to.

"Never mind," she says as Mom starts to wander over to the door. We watch her almost slip on some ice and then fumble with the doorknob for a bit and go inside.

"Why didn't you tell me?" she says, turning to me. Not accusingly. She sounds … hurt.

And now, on top of everything, I feel bad for messing this up.

"I … don't know."

"I'm sorry you have to deal with that," she says after a while, and again, I feel like maybe this whole situation can be salvaged. "Are you okay to go in?" she asks.

"Yeah. Like I said, I have to be somewhere soon anyway." Lies on top of lies. But I can't let on that I lied about that too. "I just have to grab something, then go. My dad's home." Maybe. Probably not. "He'll deal with her."

"Okay, good. I'm gonna go then." Her tone's a bit cool now.

The withdrawal has already begun.

"Take it easy," she says.

"You too," I say, for lack of anything else to say.

And with that, she turns and leaves me — for, I'm quite certain, the last time.

12

I'm lying down on a subway car bench. The train's careening wildly down the track. No way it's going to stop at the station.

It doesn't.

It's completely out of control.

I want to press the emergency strip, but I can't get up.

Suddenly I realize Mom's on the subway car too. She's wandering through it aimlessly, and suddenly she notices me.

Shit.

"There you are," she slurs, coming closer. "Been looking for you."

Suddenly at the next station, the subway comes to a skidding halt.

Good, I think, I'll get off.

But I still can't get up.

A bunch of people get on.

More and more and more.

They keep coming.

Mom's sitting on me now, and a million other people are pushing up against us.

It's hard to breathe.

The train's packed way too tightly.

This is a fire hazard, I think.

Somebody standing over me coughs. Not into his sleeve.

"Sorry, I have the virus," he says.

Noooo, I think.

"Fuck you," my mom says to him.

Or is she talking to me?

There's another cough.

Then another sneeze.

Then the whole car's coughing and sneezing.

"We're gonna die," Mom slurs. "And it's all your fault."

How is it my fault?! I want to scream, but I can't.

"Ugh, those two smell bad," someone says.

It's Molly. To Maddie?

I want to explain everything, but I can't.

I'm not sure what I'd say anyway. Telling her my mom's way too into booze, weed, and pain pills wouldn't help. That's why she pulled away.

I make myself wake up and look at the clock. It's still depressingly early, and I head to the kitchen for a late-night snack.

13

IT'S NO SURPRISE, BUT I'm a bit hurt I don't hear from Molly. If it were me, I know I'd check in by text — send a "Hey, you okay?" message. But nothing. I suspect I won't see her anymore either. There'll be no more accosting me at my locker. And we don't have any classes together, and I leave the school grounds at lunch. So that's that.

On another level, I know her withdrawal doesn't mean she's a bad person, just someone too well-adjusted to have chaos in her life in the form of a friend who lies all the time and who has an unhinged mother.

Thinking about it this way just makes me feel worse.

I tell myself again I knew this would happen, tried to avoid it happening. Didn't want to be friends with her for exactly this reason, so it's no big deal. We weren't close.

Still feels bad.

And of course, I'm filled with even more rage about my mom. Especially when I hear her yelling at her agent, Dave, again over the phone. Poor guy. He means well, but he should really give up.

The rage also extends to my dad, who doesn't seem to realize any of this affects me.

He comes home when I'm at the kitchen pantry looking for snacks to feed my empty soul. This time, when he says, "What's up?" I decide to tell him, as an experiment.

"These things happen," he says vaguely when I'm done. "You'll make new friends." Then he yawns and says, "I'm beat. Night."

Wow.

Sure, young people lose and make new friends all the time. But for these reasons? I stare after him. Do I really just overreact to everything?

I'm pretty sure I don't, but I have to rely on my own instincts about that, and I'm not at all sure I can trust those.

I DON'T IMPROVE AT driving. Get much worse, as a matter of fact. Snow and ice and skids scare the living daylights out of me. (Why didn't I wait till spring?) The city streets are an icy nightmare. Shot concentration + dangerous conditions = not a good combination.

"Holy shit, Kelsey, you're gonna need ten years of lessons," Will hoots.

Sounds about right.

And then there's the small matter of how I've been bombing my most recent algebra tests. My uni applications were in in December, but this term's marks will be forwarded too, and they're definitely going to sink me. Things are crazy competitive these days. I need help, stat.

I could find some other tutor, but I find myself texting Luca Kitescu before I can stop myself. *Hey, was thinking it's probs a good idea for me to get help with last week's algebra before we go on to new stuff...*

The answer comes pretty quickly. *Ya, probs. Tomorrow? Caf? Halfway through lunch?*

Whoa, I guess I really have to meet with him now. What was I thinking?

Scratch that. I know exactly what I was thinking. That dialing up that relationship might make me feel better about the loss of Molly's friendship. Also, that I need someone to eat lunch with. It's too damn cold to keep going to Trinity Bellwoods. Haha, not that I'll ever eat lunch with Luca Kitescu, but a girl can dream.

I delete about ten million half-composed responses and finally decide on a simple thumbs-up emoji.

Hoo boy.

I PRETEND WE'RE ON a date even though I know it's obvious to the ten thousand people who say hi to Luca during our tutoring session that I'm a client. Our table's littered with textbooks.

Appearance-wise, I'm taking my cue these days from all those celebs on the no-makeup, no-filter train. But I'm wearing great-fitting jeans and a nice puff-sleeved sweatshirt I invested in back in early January when I thought improving my appearance might also somehow improve my life. I quickly curled my hair in loose waves before leaving the house this morning and hope I look like I rolled out of bed this way.

"Thanks in advance," I say. "It's really nice of you to help."

"You're welcome." He squints and smiles at me. This was *so* not a good idea. That smile turns me stupid. And he's wearing his Clark Kent specs.

Once again, I feel uncomfortably aware that our textlationship has progressed way beyond our in-person relationship. He seems a bit distant in person. But like a good math genius, he launches into an enthusiastic summary of last week's algebra lessons. He's a really good tutor — able to simplify and explain the concepts in a way I understand. By midway through our session, a lot of stuff has become clearer. Except for whether he is, in fact, interested in me as more than a tutoring client.

"Wow," I say when we wind up, "you're really good at this. I actually get it now."

"Awesome," he says. "You're so smart. You just need to listen to your instincts, have more confidence."

"Story of my life," I say and immediately regret it. Nobody wants somebody with issues. "Anyway, thanks again. I'll let you know if I get in trouble again."

"For sure. But just a warning — I'm gonna be going private soon, once I get a couple more testimonials."

"Wow, good for you," I say. Maybe that's why he's being so friendly, I think dispiritedly. All good salespeople cultivate personal relationships, right?

"So," he says, packing up his stuff (guess this isn't going to turn into a real date after all, which I was half hoping it would, even though rumor has it he and Angel are close to being on again), "*Happily Ever After*. Chloe."

"She's evil.'

"*Evil*. Harsh."

Great. He thinks I'm harsh. Which I guess I am.

"Does evil exist?" he says. "Or is she just one of the walking wounded?"

My heart melts. *The walking wounded* — that's pretty deep. He's way deeper than Molly and everybody else think.

"Everybody's wounded," I say. "Can't blame your upbringing for your crappy behavior forever." (#NoteToSelf) I decide to change the subject. "I feel kind of bad watching it with everything happening in the world, don't you? All the shootings and such. I feel I should be doing something to help every minute of the day."

Wow, way to go, Kendler. You just sounded massively un-fun.

"Yeah, me too. But self-care and all. Don't beat yourself up for enjoying stuff. There's lots to be angry about, for sure, and we all gotta do what we can. But life's also pretty awesome. Gotta run — basketball practise. Hey, will you write me a testimonial?"

Okay, so maybe not *that* deep.

I say sure and goodbye.

DESPITE THE FACT THAT he's helped me, I decide it's too stressful having him as my tutor. I won't be able to afford him once he starts charging, anyway. Luckily, I do, in fact, get what's going on in the next few classes. I text him on the Saturday after our meeting to say his lesson was so good, I don't think I'll need him again till the next unit, if at all. I know he's probably at work — he's a part-timer at the Eaton Centre Apple Store — but he immediately sends back a thumbs-up emoji, and I can't seem to stop myself from continuing the convo. (#AfraidOfLosingContact)

Hope u get outside at lunch – weirdly nice out!

Lunch, lol, what's that

Eek, sounds Dickensian

Dickensian – like ur style

Haha, what style would that b?

Bookish, cute

Aw, TX, like ur style 2

What style would that be

Not bookish, cute

Aw thanks, gotta get back, l8r

Three days later, I text him again, using the fact that I got an A- on an algebra test as an excuse.

Hey, hope all good. Got an A- on al test!

But that's the end of that exchange.

A COUPLE DAYS LATER, I text him again. Luckily (ha), I have no friends to talk me out of it. (Makayla's gone dark, which she does every now and then.)

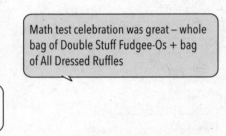

Lol, keep it classy! Sorry been MIA, so busy, talk soon!

I WAIT TWO DAYS after that exchange, then send him a bunch of lighthearted texts about my driving classes that he seems to get a kick out of, and he finally texts back. I try not to think about how I need to text him twenty-five times before he remembers I exist. But a textlationship still seems better than nothing …

Need more driving stories!

Lol, happy my failures amuse u

No failures – ur awesome, have such a great spirit

Rah, rah

So cute, gotta go, l8r

"WE ARE ALL CAPABLE of manifesting what we need and want," Dr. Ashley assures her listeners in dulcet tones. "Keep your mind free of negative thoughts. Be mindful … And be sure to treat yourself to my super relaxing lavender-goji berry essential oil!"

Haha. Hoping for stuff doesn't make it happen, essential oils give me headaches — not to mention they're ridiculously pricey — and I've tried the mindfulness thing. I suck at it.

I tell myself that despite the Molly setback and my parents, things are okay. More than okay. I've made sort-of-friends at work, and who knows, one day this thing with Luca just might become something real.

One negative: my mom barely comes out of her room now — just sleeps and coughs. I still don't know if it's smoker's cough or the virus (there's no widespread testing yet), but I'm constantly wiping everything down now. And washing my hands about a billion times a day.

I have no idea how she can live in there. I poke my head in her door one night when she's in the can to see the place filled with empty pill and booze bottles, baggies of weed, rolling papers, cartons of cigarettes, and a bunch of lighters and packs of matches. Dad's long taken over the spare bedroom, and it's no wonder.

I guess I've gotten used to the always-present, low-level smell of smoke and weed and booze all over the house, but it's a thousand times stinkier in her room.

"Get out," she mutters when she stumbles back into the room.

As always, her words are like a punch in the gut. Why am I always so shocked? (But how can a mother think it's okay to humiliate her own flesh and blood?)

And then I get mad. In my head. *Oh, I will. This is disgusting. You know, it's one thing to kill yourself, it's another to kill me and Dad. You know people get cancer from second-hand smoke, right? Do you even care?*

"Get out!" she barks again, startling me.

Her yelling gets Dad to come over, and he quickly shuts her door. "What are you doing?"

"You been in there lately? Seen what's going on?"

He sighs. "She's too far gone, Kelsey. I've tried to get her to smoke outside. She won't. "

"You haven't tried all that hard," I snap (dimly aware I'm yelling at him because I can't at her). "Afraid she'll take off if the conditions here are too tough?"

He looks a bit stunned at that, and I leap in again before he can come up with something to clap back with. "Doesn't matter how any of this affects me, does it?" Ugh, I sound so emo, but can't seem to stop myself. "Hope you're happy with your choices."

I go to my room and slam the door.

14

Now Mom's sick too, but set doc says it's just the flu. I wonder, but there's no widespread testing for C here yet

Eek. Same over here. U okay?

I'm okay – hopefully doc is right

Hope so!

How's the man?

Good tutor, lol

Just tutoring? Lol

Ya, clearly I've been imagining a big love affair, lol

Nah, he's using it as cover & is really IN LOVE WITH U 💘

Haha, don't think so. But can't figure him out. Sometimes messages are flirty, but no progress

Boys = more trouble than they're worth

Lol, probs right

How's the mom?

Worse & worse

Aw, sorry, hon

Aw, I'm sorry for *u*, wish I could help

U do help just by being there

♥

15

MY LIT TEACHER, MS. COLE, is one of those movie-type teachers. Lovely on the outside and in. The kind of person I know I'll never be. So ... serene. Never loses her temper. Doesn't seem to have one. Rare in a high school teacher — they're tested on the reg. She also knows her stuff. It's my favorite class.

One day she's discussing archetypes with us, and she reads a poem about the Minotaur creature of Greek mythology. A lively discussion about monsters ensues, and I find myself raising my hand (#WhatEven) to say, "I don't think of the Minotaur as a monster."

"Interesting," says Ms. Cole. "These figures are certainly ripe for psychoanalytic interpretation. Let's hear your take, Kelsey."

"Well, the thing was born after a disastrous hookup." I'm surprised there aren't any titters when I say "hookup." Maybe people are just shocked I'm talking. Or maybe it's down to how Cole, like all the best teachers, effortlessly commands respectful behavior. "It was unloved, neglected, mistreated, and starved. No wonder it's angry."

And no wonder I can relate — a little anyway — to the emotional aspect of the neglect. The neediness.

And, to some extent, the rage.

AFTER SCHOOL, I HEAD over to 1414 Lingerie, on Queen, to buy a new bra. (Watch out, world, I'm a full A cup now!) I'm starved by the time I leave 'cause the process takes hours. They make a v. big deal of measuring you to figure out your true size — practically throw you a party. Or maybe they were just extra nice to me 'cause no mom?

I don't feel like going home for dinner, and I'm too hungry to schlep to another neighborhood. So of course, I bump into Luca Kitescu and Will Brown at Momo Momo, the trendy new Tibetan place two doors from the lingerie store. Which I went into thinking it was the ubiquitous, un-trendy kind, as it's situated between a laundromat and a pizza place. Nope. This one's casual and cafeteria style, but insanely expensive. I'm forced to awkwardly sit with Luca and Will after shoving my 1414 bag into my tote like it's a loaded gun.

Luca looks his usual crush-worthy self. I'm overwhelmed with gratitude for having discovered, just last night on YouTube, the miracle of dryer sheets for static-y, cold-weather hair. I don't look Angel Aquino-level good, but it's the best I can do without popping a blood vessel in my eye from stress.

They're talking about driving.

"Get your license yet?" Will asks. And I'm so shocked he's actually directed a question at me, I can't think up a witty response on the spot. (Not that I can ever think up a witty response on the spot.) My driving test fell on the snowiest day of the year, and I couldn't get out of a skid and flunked unceremoniously.

"Taking more lessons," I mutter before taking a bite of my (single) momo and chewing for longer than strictly necessary.

"Ha, no surprise," he says.

"Don't be an asshole," Luca says.

My cheeks heat. Nothing like being laughed at in front of your crush.

They talk about getting wasted at various parties, which makes me feel at once awkward and inexperienced — I've never even been to a high school party — but also like a very old soul. (Given what I see daily, I'm pretty sure I never want to go to one.) Then Will changes the subject to the latest MacBook he just blew a couple grand on. Then he asks me kind of computer I have, and I practically whisper, "An Asus."

"You kidding me?"

"Being an asshole again," Luca says.

"That all you're eating?" Will looks at my half-eaten momo. "Hannah Kendler's your mom, right? Wasn't she on TV? Can't you afford a meal?"

My face flushes again. "She was on TV, yes. 'Was' being the operative word."

"Where you going on break?" Will asks Luca, apparently deciding that since I have to watch my money, I'm unworthy of attention. (I'm suddenly certain he's the spawn of a landlord specializing in renovictions.)

"My uncle's cabin."

"Nice," he says in a tone that says he doesn't really think so. "Whistler for me. Wish I was going somewhere warm." He gives me a questioning look. Wow, he's being really magnanimous now, letting me talk.

"Home sweet home," I say.

"Maryjane time," Will announces, getting up. I've bored him. He's already scarfed his huge momo plate, thank the universe. "Follow if you want to partake."

Neither Luca nor I follow.

"So," I say awkwardly. He's as awkward as I am, if not more so — he just doesn't seem to know it. Which makes him un-awkward. So unfair.

"So," he says.

"So. Uncle with a cabin up north. Sweet."

"Yeah," he says. "It's awesome. I ski in the winter, do standup paddleboard in the summer. Ever do it?"

I almost laugh. "Nope."

"You can take a lesson at Ashbridges Bay in the summer. Then we can do it together sometime."

"Really? Cool. Maybe I will." (*Stay calm. He's talking about a friend date. And it'll probably never happen.*)

He takes a couple bites of a momo. "So. *Happily Ever After.* Cassandra. Dark horse. Ethan's in love."

"Hope he sees through her soon."

"You think she's evil too?"

Yikes. He thinks I'm a cynical bitch. But I can't help saying, "Didn't you see what she said to Tess at the house?"

"It's late in the season. Natural for her nerves to be shot."

"I think *you're* the one who's in love, my friend."

He grins. "Final four next week. We should have a party."

"I'm down." *Keep cool.*

His phone buzzes. He looks at it and says, "Shit, gotta go. See ya."

And with that, he's gone.

Is it my crappy parental situation that makes me crave attention from unavailable people?

I wait a couple minutes, then go too so I don't have to see Will when he gets back.

And arrive home just in time to see the 'rents leaving the house in an ambulance. My dad's text: *Saw you. Mom's fine. Don't worry. Don't wait up.*

Right. As if I'll be able to sleep.

APPARENTLY "FINE" MEANS BLACKING out for only a few minutes.

Those two are beyond hopeless.

I suffer through more snow- and ice-driving with Will and Maya doppelgangers and don't improve at all. Possibly, I'm worse. (#EvenMoreAnxious)

"I paid for all those goddamn lessons for you to quit?" Mom yells one night when she stumbles into the kitchen to hear me tell Dad I don't want to think about driving for a while.

Oh, great, now it's starting a whole *thing*.

"Sorry I wasted your money," I say, rising from the dining

room table. She responds by hacking up a lung. "And you should probably stay in your room," I find the guts to say. "You probably have the virus."

"She doesn't have the virus!" Dad says.

"How do you know? Are you a doctor now?" I say, proving to him, once again, that I'm just another emo teen.

Dad sighs deeply. "They screened her at the hospital."

Oh. There's still no widespread testing, but of course they're doing it for coughers in hospitals …

One less thing I have to worry about, anyway.

Back in my room, I start a text convo with my work buds about how our soft serve flavors are kind of boring. They aren't friends in the strict sense of the word, but they remind me I'm not completely on my own.

Least, I hope not.

THERE'S SO MUCH SNOW and ice on the ground, I have to leave the house at the crack of dawn to get to school on time.

And I still get there late on a day Ms. Cole assigns us a persuasive essay and gives me a concerned look when I come in. I look at the board. We can use, as the source material/topic, any work we've read so far this term. I already know I'm going to do mine on the Minotaur poem.

After she gets a million questions on everything she just explained ("What's a persuasive essay?" "How long should it be?" "When's this due?"), she dismisses us and calls me over to her desk. "Is everything all right with you, Kelsey?" she asks when I approach.

There's so much warmth in her voice, and it's so nice somebody cares enough to ask — not that I'm under any illusion I'm special to her, either — I feel my eyes well up. (Again. Le sigh.)

I can't afford to cry in school, so I just wait a second till I think I can talk without my voice shaking, then say, "Yeah, I'm good. Sorry, gotta run."

At lunch, I drag myself to Trinity Bellwoods, where I freeze my ass off, but where at least I can cry anonymously.

A NEW DESSERT PLACE has opened around the block called Hotties, with super attractive staffers serving twenty kinds of hot chocolate in a club-like space complete with DJ and dance floor. Seems more suited to the entertainment district, but it's the brainchild of a pop star from Parkdale who wanted it here, and his gamble paid off — it's jammed around the clock.

Though I'm worried about my now extremely sparse hours at Soft Spot, I do appreciate the time alone or with one other person in the store. I mostly clean stuff, and the scrubbing is kind of therapeutic. Plus, when I'm on with quiet types like Ruby or Lee (who gives me the silent treatment whenever I tell him I haven't watched *The Wire* yet), I can message people all day. People like Luca Kitescu. I'm aware continuing our textlationship is a terrible idea (will just get more attached), but I can't help myself. Every text gives me a hit of much-needed dopamine, and I'm still holding out hope it'll turn into something real.

> Saw ur tutoring service poster! Congrats! No more freesplaining!

> Haha, ya, thanks. So many customers already

Ya I bet – the ones u lured with freebies, then hit with the now-u-have-to-pay announcement

Busted, lol

Sadly I can't afford u

Would be weird tutoring u anyway

How come?

'Cause we're so … friendly

But mostly in text …

I know. So crazy busy – school & sports & tutoring & still working at the Apple store

Wow, that's a lot, I'm just doing school and Soft Spot … feel like a loser, lol

Nah ur smart

Lol, cute u think so after seeing my sub-par math skills

Haha, I know ur smart – such funny texts

Lol, everybody's funny in texts

Not true

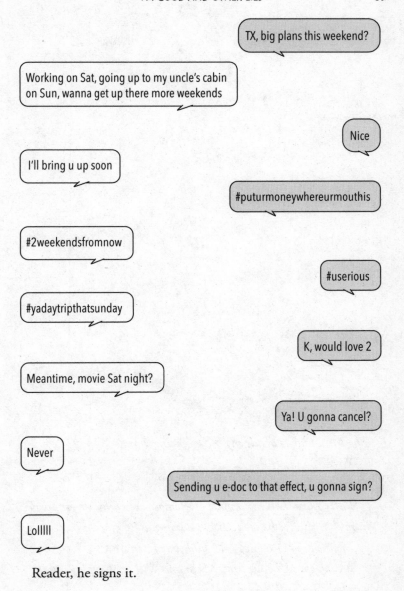

TX, big plans this weekend?

Working on Sat, going up to my uncle's cabin on Sun, wanna get up there more weekends

Nice

I'll bring u up soon

#puturmoneywhereurmouthis

#2weekendsfromnow

#userious

#yadaytripthatsunday

K, would love 2

Meantime, movie Sat night?

Ya! U gonna cancel?

Never

Sending u e-doc to that effect, u gonna sign?

Lolllll

Reader, he signs it.

16

The Minotaur is beside my bed, wearing a bra.

Weird.

Steam is coming out of its nostrils.

Enter Luca, holding a plate of momos. "You'd better get away from that thing," he says. "Looks dangerous."

I want to say I would if I could, but I can't.

A car pops up beside him. Maya and Will are hanging out the windows and call to him.

"Hey," he says to me, "wanna come?"

I want to say yeah, even though I don't, really, 'cause Maya and Will, but I figure between them and the Minotaur, they're the lesser of the two evils.

I can't move, 'course, but the Minotaur still thinks I'm gonna leave and now it looks … sad.

I want to ask it why it's so sad, but I can't.

Luca hops in the car. "Let's go to Hotties," he says.

I want to tell him he was supposed to go on a date with me, but I can't.

But he seems to know what I was about to say — he hangs out the window to look at me and shrugs.

Then they zoom off, laughing.

As they drive off, I hear Maya cough.

I watch them go, then look back at the Minotaur.

It doesn't look sad anymore.

It's super angry-looking and snorting loudly.

And no longer wearing the bra. Nothing comical about it now.

Then it starts coughing. Hard and loud.

Then it's howling in pain.

Wake up, wake up, wake up, I order myself.

I finally do. And tell myself the dream was silly, that Luca likes me and wants to start something.

And that minotaurs aren't real, and nobody I know has the virus. Yet.

17

NEEDLESS TO SAY, CHELSEA, with whom I'm on a shift just before my date, is super excited. I've told her a little about my textlationship with Luca. "I knew it would happen! You two are soul mates! What movie are you seeing? Are you gonna get dinner before or after? What are you going to wear? Omigod, I feel like your mother!"

You're more my mother than my mother, I think. Obviously I haven't told my actual mother. Or my father. Neither of them would care.

I tell her we're hitting the Skyline Restaurant before the movie — *The Grudge*, a horror flick #GoodForCuddling, according to Luca. I plan to wear those great-fitting jeans, my favorite cold shoulder sweater, and a decent imitation of a Canada Goose puffer. Chelsea squeals and claps and orders me to send her a mirror selfie before I leave my house ...

IT'S FINALLY HAPPENING, I think when I spot him at the Skyline, a beloved Parkdale diner that's always packed. He looks gorgeous in blue jeans, a white T-shirt, black V-neck pullover and slim fitting black puffer. "Hi," he says, a look of appreciation on his face, "you look great."

"Hi," I say, going in for a hug. "Thanks. Same."

We're pointed to a table, and I fairly float to it beside Luca. Once seated, we talk about *Happily Ever After* and then we both order burgers and fries. (I'm happy to splurge tonight!)

"More stuff in common," Luca says with a smile, and I order myself not to stare at that gorgeous jawline.

Through dinner, we talk about school and our jobs and then we walk, huddled close, to the theater. (He loves long walks too!) The movie is funny and scary and during it we share a kiss that I think might be the best kiss in the history of kissing (*please don't let him be a virus carrier*) — until the one he plants on me at the end of the night, in front of my house, which is longer and deeper and comes with soft groans from both of us.

I can't believe he wants this as much as I do.

"We need to do more of that," I murmur when we break apart. Why does anyone who has someone to kiss and cuddle need to drink or do drugs? What a high!

"Definitely." He smiles gorgeously. "Next week. We'll go to my uncle's cabin on Sunday. He won't be there, and he doesn't have kids. I have the place to myself a lot of the time."

Amazing, I think in bed a half hour later. I'm sure we'll do more than cuddle at his uncle's cabin. I might even lose my V-card before uni, which I thought for sure was an un-meet-able goal!

And it just gets better. Once I'm home, he sends a text saying, *Hey, that was really nice. Would like 2 make it a habit.*

I can't even believe it. I'm actually getting something I desperately wanted but didn't dare hope for.

Same, I text back. *Is this really happening?*

Yup, gonna be awesome.

He texts me photos of his uncle's cabin and says *Next week!* And not even my mom blacking out and banging her head on the corner of her nightstand and my dad having to take her to emerg again can bring me down.

I'M TRYING TO WRANGLE my mom inside from the sidewalk in front of our house one day when he suddenly appears in front of us.

Oh my freaking god, is all I can think. It's the exact same thing that happened with Molly. Mom barely leaves her room, and the two times she does …

"Need some help?" he asks. I can tell he thinks she's harassing me.

"Who are you?" Mom mumbles. "Hey, you're cute. You know her? Just a warning, she's no fun!" She giggles at this, and I want to sink into the ground.

Now Luca freezes. "This … your mom?"

"Yeah," I whisper. "You go on," I manage to add. "I'll get her inside."

"I can help …"

"Better it's just me. Lots of practise, text you later," I say, not wanting him to see any more and dimly aware this might be the last time he talks to me.

I can't have nice things.

18

Mom and Dad are both standing over me, yelling about how I'm a screwup.

I try to tell them I'm not the screwup, they're the screwups, and I even have a boyfriend now. But I can't.

Now Makayla's mom is at the side of my bed, coughing.

I try to tell her to cough into her elbow, and that she probably has COVID, but I can't.

Then Mom and Dad start coughing too. Quietly at first, then louder, until they're doubled over in pain.

Then the rats burst out of the walls again.

Hundreds and hundreds of them.

Gross.

They start gnawing on the bottoms of Mom's and Dad's and Mikayla's mom's pants, then begin to climb up their bodies.

The coughs turn to shrieks.

They're all completely covered now.

Super gross.

My phone buzzes. It's propped on my chest, and I can see a text coming in from Luca: Hey, Kels, I've realized I want 2 get back with Angel — give it a real shot this time.

He can't have just said that, is my first reaction. But I keep looking at the text, and it doesn't disappear.

I can't move my arms or hands to pick up the phone and respond.

More words: U r amazing. I was confused. Please try 2 understand.

I wanted to be the one you took the shot with, I think, brokenhearted.

I wish u health, happiness, and joy, says his next text.

Sounds like a holiday card, I think, stung, and vow to delete his contact information and our entire text history as soon as I wake up.

19

BUT IN THE MORNING, there are no such texts. Only a super sweet one:

Hey, Kels, my uncle — the one with the cabin — had a bad drinking prob for a while. Not sure what's going on with ur mom, but I can send u links 2 places that helped him.

Ur so sweet! Thank u! Ya, it's something like that. I refrain from telling him it's alcohol, weed, *and* pills. *Def send me the links, though we'd have to get her 2 admit she has a problem first!* I've no doubt both Mom and Dad would just brush off an intervention attempt. Another intervention attempt. (There was that time I tried to say something and she called me a nag ...)

I'm on such a high after that, not even Mom and Dad's increased fighting can get me down.

"It's a damn pigsty in here, Hannah! Is this really how you want to live?"

"You don't like it, then get outta here. Not like you're a real husband anyway. Goddamn screwup." Cough, cough.

"Anybody living with you is a goddamn screwup, Hannah."

Interesting how he lets her know she's unstable when he talks to her, but won't acknowledge it when he talks to me.

Their argument dramatically increases in volume, as do the rat-scratching sounds — they sound like they're in the walls of my room now.

I make a mental note to buy a pair of noise-canceling headphones.

A SHOP VISIT FROM Chelsea's dad doesn't get me down either, as it normally would.

When she introduces us, he says, "Hi, Kelsey, lovely to meet you," in a deep English accent. He and Chelsea's mom are both literature professors. Smiling, he adds, "I had to come here to see her. She's been so busy. Do your parents get to see you much these days?"

I just smile and shrug.

"Omigod," Chelsea says after her dad buys a butterscotch dip, they exchange some more adorable small talk, and he says goodbye. "You're totally in love, aren't you?"

"Well, I don't wanna get ahead of myself ..."

"That's so awesome." She sighs. "Love really does make the world go 'round!"

Just then, a regular customer comes in and Chelsea squeals, "Omigod, I love your purse! You're so cool and stylish!"

Something else that might have broken me a little in the BL

(Before Luca) times. I would have thought, I'm not special, she talks to everyone that way.

Purse girl seems sad today, and Chelsea urges her to order chocolate-dipped banana. "It's like a hug on a plate!" she says. "Just what the doctor ordered!"

Sure, I would have thought before, in some alternate universe where shit can be helped by ice cream.

But now I have Luca. Who thinks I'm special. And that's made me the happiest girl in the world.

It occurs to me that, just as I made the Luca thing happen, I could try to turn my co-workers into actual friends. Work friends would be ideal — we'd likely just go places in a group after work and not hang at each other's houses.

"Hey," I say, when we're close to closing, "anybody up for a movie when we're done?" Today, it's me, Quinn, Chelsea, and Ruby. We've mostly been chopping candy. It's super slow. There's another new kid in town, MERingue, a vegan, mermaid-themed meringue place. The vegans have been slowly taking over Parkdale, even calling it "Vegandale," to the ire of the area's non-vegan inhabitants. Soft Spot's days seem very numbered.

"No can do," Quinn says. "I have an audition. Family Channel show. They're talking to Vanessa Hudgens about playing my mom."

I grin despite myself. "Spoken like you've already bagged the role. No shortage of confidence."

"Gotta believe in yourself, baby."

I look at Ruby and Chelsea. "You two?"

"Sorry, I can't," Ruby says. She puts her head down and focuses on pulling off a hangnail.

Okay, well, that one was a long shot.

"Aw, sorry, hon, I have a school play rehearsal," says Chelsea.

"No worries."

It's not like I actually expected this to work. But the blow isn't as bad 'cause Luca.

But wait. A second later, Chelsea says, "Let's try and coordinate a night we *can* all make it."

And whaddya know, we do!

"ONE DAY," SAYS DOC Ashley that night, "all those nos will turn into yeses and that will be a great day! Congratulations if that's already happened!"

"Why, thank you," I say aloud, smiling.

"You deserve a treat — for trying, for putting yourself out there, whether it paid off this time or not! Don't forget to check out my online store and tell all your friends about my podcast and shop! You'll love my lavender-goji berry essential oil blend!"

I do deserve a treat! And maybe Doc Ashley's essential oils won't give me headaches! I'll order a bottle as soon as the show's over!

She goes on to say that life has three pillars — work, family, and love — and you're doing well if two out of those three pillars are solid. (Wow, she really is a smart one — I've definitely been under-estimating her!) Both my work life (school, Soft Spot) and my love life are going swimmingly. The family pillar's still a broken mess, but tonight, with the knowledge that a) Luca and I are probably going to be bf and gf and b) I'm going to have real friends soon, I go to bed on a high.

Not that I'm still not visited by sleep paralysis demons.

Or that the next day, everything doesn't completely turn to shit ...

20

Tom Hanks & his wife have it. & I'm pretty sure everyone on Mom's set – including her – has it too

Oh, shit!

They're finally getting tested this aft

Fingers crossed she's neg …

TX. She's still coughing & sleeping most of the day. How are *u*?

I'm good! Luca and I r a bit of a thing!

The tutor? Ahhhh, that's amazing! U deserve All the Luv!

Aw, thank uuuuu! But I'm so sorry ur mom's sick! Must b so scary!

It is! & the orange man still wants to hide what's really going on …

Ugh, so awful. They should be testing more people here 2 …

By the time our governments get their act together, there'll be massive community spread …

Can't think about that!

Right? Gotta go – take it easy! Yay, luv! Luv u!

U 2 and love u 2! Crossing my fingers for ur mom!!!!!!

PART TWO
Lockdown
—

A.K.A. My Worst Nightmare

21

SUDDENLY, THERE ARE A whole bunch of hospitalizations and deaths related to COVID-19.

Public health officials start talking about how it may take school and business closures to get things under control — and something called bubbling, which means only interacting with the people you live with.

Heaven forbid. Being stuck with my parents 24/7 is pretty much my worst nightmare.

Not to mention a lockdown will kill my pending relationship with Luca — our cabin weekend's coming up! And I have to solidify those work friendships ...

It won't happen, I tell myself firmly. Our leaders care too

much about the economy — they wouldn't want to sacrifice it, even if closing everything is the right thing to do.

But then all non-essential businesses are ordered to close.

I text Luca, *Guess our trip to the cabin's a no-go* 😞, and all he says is *Ya, sucks!*

Soon after that, he texts me two links — one to CAMH (the nearby Centre for Addiction and Mental Health) and another to a private rehab place just north of Toronto. I guess he forgot to send them to me till now, and I never reminded him (knowing my mom will never seek help). There's no accompanying text with the links. And he doesn't answer my thank-you message.

My texts to my work friends get similar, one-word responses. ("Sucks!" "Unbelievable!")

There's still school, I tell myself (because I can't let myself think they'll take that away from me too).

And then we're told not to return from March Break.

BEFORE I BEGIN HIBERNATING at home, I finally buy those noise-canceling headphones.

It doesn't take long for me to start feeling a constant pit of dread in my stomach. The future is now a big, uncertain blur. I feel so ... unmoored. School and work were anchors for me, I realize. Shitty anchors much of the time, but anchors, nonetheless. And it's clear I'm back to being alone, floating away toward that uncertain future, without a single person to help me sail ...

NOR DOES IT TAKE long for all kinds of think pieces to appear online about who's faring well mentally and who isn't. It comes as absolutely no surprise whatsoever to me that the people with strong support systems are the ones doing well and the people without them aren't.

I have no support system.

I'm sure my co-workers and Luca are as freaked out as I am, and I can't blame them for not checking in — I never got the chance to really solidify any of those relationships. But I still can't help feeling angry and frustrated re: their ghosting. Clearly, they all have other sources of support, but I don't.

I MAKE MYSELF THINK of positives. At least everybody's stuck at home — no more FOMO! I tell myself I'll focus on my schoolwork. And immerse myself in career research. Back in December, I applied to general uni programs because I had no idea what I wanted to do with my life. (Other kids complain about their parents' attempts to brainwash them. I *wish* my parents would give me some kind — any kind — of career guidance.)

I try to stop the panic-stricken thoughts about how, due to the virus, I may not, in fact, be headed to uni in September — that this year might be ruined, and maybe next year too.

That absolutely cannot happen.

AND IT ISN'T LONG before "remote learning," instituted after the break, becomes a total shit show. There's no more talk of teacher strikes, and our Minister of Education seems downright gleeful about e-learning. I get the feeling he thinks it doesn't require teachers.

I've never been a great independent learner. Need demos and instructors so I can ask questions. Hope I get that.

Don't worry, says the first email from our principal. *Your learning will proceed unabated. Look out for detailed instructions on how we will be guiding you.*

Guiding you. That doesn't bode well. That sounds like we're on our own. No actual lessons.

Sure enough, my email is soon flooded with assignment instructions. I get the feeling nobody knows quite how to proceed. (I'm sure the ministry's giving them zero guidance.) And every teacher wants us to get on different online platforms — Zoom, Skype, Google Meet …

Dammit, I'm going to have to figure out all the platforms and remember to constantly check my email as well as all the places on all the platforms where assignments and answers to questions might be posted. Even with all my checking, I'm sure stuff will fall through the cracks. I'm pretty tech-stupid even though I'm of the "digital native" generation. Nothing seems intuitive to me.

Sure enough, I spend most of my days tearing my hair out over tech issues. What might have helped — having someone demo things for me in person — isn't possible.

Dad chooses — of course — to remove himself from the whole situation by "working" in the broken-down backyard shed. He'd rather freeze in there than spend time with his wife and kid. If I asked for his help, he'd probably just say something like, "Didn't they teach you this stuff?" and wouldn't believe me if I said no. Being the most distant of dads, he has absolutely no idea what I have or haven't learned.

Best to avoid that situation altogether.

And while I'm lucky enough to have my own computer (don't know how families with one computer will do it), our Wi-Fi's newly spotty. When I ask Dad about that, he says he's cut some costs and I have to nab a neighbor's signal.

"Which will make their Wi-Fi spotty," I say. So sketchy.

He throws up his hands. "Kelsey, it is what it is. Lots of kids have it worse than you. Deal."

I send my algebra, bio, and French teachers questions about emailed lessons and assignments I don't understand. And hear back from one of them after several nudges. Ugh, I'm sure all the teachers are overwhelmed too, but I'm the one with uni — my ticket outta here — on the line.

One night, after giving up and scrolling Insta, I learn the private school kids are getting live lessons on Zoom. I'm so jealous.

Not that that would be great for me either. Mom would probably wander into the frame and become an instant meme.

On Insta (yeah, me, masochist), I see Luca post a pic of some books with the heading, *Hitting the books #c-19*. And I see somebody I don't know comment that they're starting a student forum since teachers are mostly incommunicado. Okay, I think, surely someone or a few someones on the student forum will be able to answer my questions.

It takes me a bit of time to figure out where to find the forum. When I finally do, I post my questions.

Nothing.

I politely post them again a couple days later. By this time, it's been confirmed that the ministry isn't planning to green-light "synchronous learning" — the official term, I learn, for live video-teaching.

I'm completely panicked.

And then I get a private message from the person running

the forum saying, *Hi, Kelsey. Sorry, but we're making the forum private. Too overwhelming when it's public. Too many people. Good luck!*

A week in and I'm already completely worn down.

ADD TO ALL THAT the joy that is sheltering in place with the 'rents. And neighbors who scream 'round the clock now. I have no idea why Mom's gone so bananas about the shutdown — it's not like she left the house much before — but now she's constantly yelling about how she's stuck with two pills (nice) and how she can't take it anymore (same, lady, same).

I've never heard — or heard of — any other parent talking about their family members this way.

Dad quickly realized it's way too cold to work in the shed, and when he's not screaming at her from the dining room table to be quiet (those 'phones don't work), he's pounding on the wall to get the neighbors to be quiet — to no avail. His nerves frayed, he barks orders at me whenever I leave my room for food or to go to the can — to wash dishes, sweep, do laundry, etc. He's finally losing his cool — at my expense. I have to furiously comply because if I suggested a chore wheel or something, he'd say something about how he's taking care of this entire family, thank you very much. Which isn't even true — we're living off Mom's rapidly depleting savings. He isn't eligible for the government payments to people who lost work in the shutdowns.

"Hannah, shut it!" he yells at her one day, after a scream-y rant.

"I can't stand this," I mutter, coming out of the can.

"You too!" he says sharply.

Right.

22

She's gone, K. Happened so fast. I'm
freaking out here

What???? Holy shit, M, I'm so sorry!
Can't believe it! Can I call?

No, I'm just hopping on a plane – a private
one. Actor friend of mom thinks we can get over
the closed border. Going to my dad's. Am in shock

Holy shit, I'm so, so sorry. Let
me know when ur here!

TX. Can't believe this is happening

Omigod

She tested positive & was isolating, seemed like she was getting better, then had trouble breathing, was rushed to hospital & three hours later, she was gone – I couldn't even see her

I don't even know what 2 say, M. Whatever u need, I'm here

TX. I was such a shit daughter

No u weren't! Not at all!

Told her she was selfish for bringing me here

Ur entitled 2 ur feelings!

Never even told her I loved her

It's hard to love some people and u don't have to feel guilty if u didn't

I know but

I know

Wish things could've been different

I hear u

I don't even know what's happening with her body. Not sure we can bring her back cuz of virus …

Oh wow

& now I have to live with my dad & Hayley

Sucks!

None of this feels real

Love u, M 🖤

Luv u too, K, TX for being there

ANYTIME – call me when u get 2 ur dad's once ur settled if u want!

K, might, but u know me and the phone 🖤

No worries – whatever u feel like, am here for u 🖤

23

SHE DOESN'T CALL.

I call her a couple times, then switch to texting, but she doesn't respond anytime over the next few days. I figure maybe it's all been too much for her, that maybe she's had some sort of breakdown.

I feel terrible.

I can't believe her mom's gone. I wasn't a fan (met her a few times and she talked nonstop about herself at all times), but still.

I hope Makayla gets in touch at some point.

But what if she doesn't?

What if she's decided it's not worth the effort of keeping in touch with me or being my friend, given I'm clear across town now?

I tell myself that's ridiculous and demonstrably untrue — her texts are always loaded with love-yous and heart emojis. (All teens overuse those, says the annoying voice in my head ...)

Holy shit, what if she caught the virus from her mom and now she's sick? The thought hits me like a ton of bricks.

What if she dies? They're saying young people aren't getting as seriously sick as older people, but her mom was pretty young too ...

M isn't dead or dying, I tell myself. She's just overwhelmed with grief — even if she didn't love (or like) her mom. I feel terrible for her.

And also for me because Luca and all my work friends have gone radio silent, and Makayla's silence is one more loss. One more anchor that's disappeared.

I've never felt so alone.

ONE DAY THERE'S AN email that promises our grades won't slip below the ones we were holding before the shutdown, and I'm overcome with relief.

At the same time, I realize I can hoard snack food from the pantry in my room and not emerge for meals. Nobody will miss me. Nobody here's using the lockdown as an opportunity for "bonding" — we still don't regularly eat together. Holing up in my room will significantly limit harmful exposure to the people I live with.

You know how it's pretty much a guarantee that you get sick when you go on vacation? Because your body realizes it can finally let go?

That happens to me as soon as I make the decision to ignore the schoolwork.

The day I quit school, my body lets me know exactly how much stress I've been under. I get a killer headache, and an exhaustion like I've never felt before washes over me.

Then I think, uh-oh, it might not be run-of-the-mill, stress-related sickness, but the virus. I'm not coughing, but I've heard that some people just get tired and achy.

Shit. What if I die? They're saying young people don't get it in a serious way, but maybe they just haven't seen those cases yet …

I call my doctor. Who I don't get to talk to. Her receptionist sounds harried when I ask if I can get tested.

"There still aren't enough kits in the city," she says. "So we're telling people that unless you've traveled recently, or been in contact with a confirmed case, or are having trouble breathing, just stay home and do the things you would do if you had the flu. Take Tylenol if you have a fever, drink fluids, and get plenty of rest."

I stupidly didn't take my temperature before calling. I take it now and am relieved to see I don't have a fever.

Just a stress headache after all.

I've always resisted taking pills, even Tylenols. I never wanted to rely on substances like my mom — not even a little bit. But tonight I grab a headache pill from the medicine cabinet in the bathroom.

And feel woozy by the time I'm in my bedroom.

I head back to the bathroom, stepping carefully, and once there, I take the lid off the Tylenol bottle and look carefully at a pill I take out.

Dammit, it's not a Tylenol. It's Oxy.

More proof she's taking more than Melnick prescribed. She probably got this shit on the street from some scumbag who put the pills in a Tylenol bottle. Why did she put it in the medicine cabinet? What a disaster.

But maybe not, I find myself thinking a few minutes later. (Unless it's laced with something, which I decide to believe it isn't.) Maybe I need to … not feel things for a while. Just in the short term. Until the worst of the all-alone feelings pass. (Will they ever?) Until the lockdown is over. Until the virus is under control.

It's okay to accept help, I tell myself. Really, my policy of never taking anything 'cause of Mom is kind of stupid. Cutting off my nose to spite my face. I'm probably clinically depressed. I need something to take the edge off these hard, hard days of being trapped at home, the only upside of which is that Mom's finally quit screaming and is practically comatose in her room now — hopefully just from regular old drug abuse and not the virus.

I know enough not to get hooked. I'm not her.

It'll never be a problem.

I SLEEP LIKE A baby and don't get up till two the next day. Nobody checks on me, and I go back to sleep.

When I finally get up around five, I'm hungry. I dig into the snacks I brought to my room and contemplate taking another pill. I need to do something. Bleakness hangs like a dark fog over this place.

It's just temporary. Till I feel better. Till the world normalizes. Then I'll ease off.

Only soon, I decide not to set an easing-off date.

And then, on top of being lonely and unlovable, I have to face the fact that I'm just as much a screwup as my mom is.

I TRIED. I REALLY did. But life seems intent on beating me up. I don't know how others find it so easy. For me it's such a slog. Has been as long as I can remember. I'm tired of fighting.

Getting through the day is much easier when I feel out of it. I like the buzz. Life's rough, and I have no family I can count on, no friends to pump me up, it's insanely cold and stormy outside so even walks are out, and the world is a dumpster fire.

I have no idea how I got through life before, and I try not to think about how I'll never be able to go back.

DR. ASHLEY'S RESPONSE TO the lockdown is to quote the Dalai Lama.

"World peace begins with inner peace." (What on earth do world peace and inner peace have to do with the pandemic?) She sounds not quite herself on this episode. Her voice is considerably higher and tighter. Trouble in paradise? These days, apparently, even solid couples are feeling the stress and lashing out at each other ...

Nah, impossible for someone like her to have trouble coping.

Unless she's caught the virus.

"We can't fix the world until we fix ourselves."

Wow. Why did I ever think she made sense? Surely protests and voting reforms are more likely to "fix the world" than meditation and aromatherapy.

I stop listening to her when a ping notifies me of a text on the work group loop.

It's late, and, in addition to popping a pill, I've snuck a mug of wine 'cause it's getting harder and harder to get the high I got off the pill that first time.

Haha, of course I'm totally wasted when Chelsea finally decides to start group texting again. Maybe I just won't answer. It's nice that she — they — are finally getting in touch, but now I know they're completely untrustworthy …

How's everybody doing? Just over here creating magical creatures! In drops an amazing sketch of a flying cat. *I hereby challenge u to come up with ur own — in ten minutes! We all still have Finger Paint on our phones, right?*

Lol, Finger Paint, says Lee. *Try Procreate on my iPad.*

Showoff! says Chelsea.

Quinn says, *Wow, ur good! I can't draw! Gotta go — on a call!*

I can't draw either — will watch, says Kira.

Lee's the next to drop a sketch. Of a dog with fins. Super detailed.

Nice! Chelsea says.

Y'all r so good! That's Ruby. *Here's mine — don't laugh!* Ruby's pic consists of about ten strokes, but it's pretty good — of a chicken with a fish head.

That's great, Ruby! says Veer. Aw, he's sweet. If untrustworthy.

I'm extremely un-tech-y, but I do like to doodle, and do, in fact, still have Finger Paint on my phone. So screw it, I'll give it a try. Might be nice to do something different.

I do a quick sketch of a monster with a human head. (Me? My mom?)

I try to send it to the group text.

I seem to have forgotten how.

Finally I remember.

Here's urs, I say a minute later. *Oops, haha, meant min. Uh, mine.*

Nobody responds, and I'm starting to get ticked off when Chelsea says, *Did u send it yet? I don't see anything.*

No! I mean ya! Haha, I did. A kid with a monster head. No, a monster with a kid head! Here it is again!

Still no response.

In the meantime, here's mine, says Veer. His is amazing — a mouse with elephant ears. Really detailed.

U a showeff too, I say. *Oops, showoff.*

Nobody responds to that either.

My head feels like it's stuffed with cotton.

Sleep now, bye, I say.

I'm a bit surprised when Kira texts me privately almost immediately. *So … U weren't making a lot of sense just now. Times r tough. U okay?*

Ya, I'm good. I have to focus really hard to spell that right even though it's my go-to answer. *U off drugs?* I write, taking a teensy bit of pleasure in the joke. *All of a sudden ur Ms. Observant.*

Ha, actually ya I am

Wow, I say, *good for u.*

Now u gotta promise me u'll take care of urself.

Don't worry 'bout me, I'm good, am always good.

On the surface, anyway. In the past, whatever was going on in my life, I always dragged my butt to school, to work. And never let anybody know what was going on at home. Dad would've had a fit.

U sure? U don't seem like urself …

Who do I seem like? Another joke I'm pretty proud of under the circumstances.

But this one doesn't land. She doesn't respond and after a second, writes, *Sounds like ur under the influence of something. Trust me, I get the need to take the edge off. But it can get out of control really fast.*

She waits a minute before continuing. I guess for a response from me. Which she doesn't get.

I go to these online meetings. I can send u the link.

Don't need meetings, got a lot going on rn.

I'm tired from focusing so hard on spelling everything right. She isn't being a friend, she's being an annoying reformed druggie. Who clearly has some kind of sixth sense about when someone else is under the influence.

She doesn't text for a few seconds, then says, *Well, good thing u don't have to be around knives these days.*

I say bye, but not before saying, *Now u know how I felt!* which doesn't make me feel even one little bit better.

I HAVE NOTHING GOING on. Nothing but curling up in bed and drinking and drugging myself into near-oblivion.

"HEALTHY LIVING," SAYS BOLT in an email. "Good sleep hygiene and eating right are important, and so is daily exercise, even when we're at home. Aim for thirty to sixty minutes' worth. Every day."

Yeah, no.

24

Makayla and her mom are standing beside my bed.

Death is here too — a tall, shadowy figure in a dark cloak.

I want to warn them, but I can't.

Death lifts an arm, quietly and elegantly covering them with her cloak.

I want to scream, but I can't.

When Death drops her arm again, they're gone.

Now the Soft Spot crowd's here, looking at me and whispering.

Death is still here. They don't seem to notice.

I want to warn them too, but I can't.

Death draws her cloaked arm over Lee and Kira, and when she drops her arm again, they're gone.

The others don't notice.

Didn't you see that? I want to scream, but I can't.

Chelsea and Ruby are next to go.

Veer is left, looking at me. He seems sad.

He still hasn't noticed Death, who has her eye on him now.

No, don't take him too, I want to plead with her, but I can't.

Death gives me a pitying look, as if to say she's sorry for taking everyone away from me, and then she obliterates Veer.

Looking back at me, she shrugs and moves closer.

Wake up, wake up, wake up, I order myself.

And I do, just in the nick of time.

25

THE WEATHER CONTINUES TO suck.

Kira texts again.

Just checkin' in. How u doing?

I'm great, I say.

Not.

Veer sends a message that doesn't require an answer. *Thinking of u. Hope u r okay.*

He probably sent that to everybody.

Then Ms. Cole texts to ask me how I'm doing. Says she tried emailing, but I didn't respond — maybe it went to my spam? Aw, she's so sweet. I don't know what to tell her, so just shut off my phone and go back to sleep.

IT SUCKS TO HAVE tasted friendship and love and then lost them. Despite their occasional texts, the work peeps have proved I'm not among their nearest and dearest — not even close. And Luca's gone completely dark.

Pandemic aside, how do people do it? You get to know and care about people and then they're just … gone.

Actually, I can't put the pandemic aside. All the losses hurt extra-much because they came right before the shutdown, leaving me all alone, without a soul to lean on.

"EVERYTHING HAPPENS FOR A reason!" Dr. Ashley trills.

Ugh, seriously? What about mass murders, concentration camps for kids, terminal cancer, leprosy …

"Y'all are the best, but don't forget I need your help to keep helping you! Don't forget to check out the online store — we still have aromatherapy sanitizer in stock! Send me a receipt photo for discounts and also a monetary reward if one of your contacts becomes an online ambassador for positivity! Spread the word!"

THE ONLY THING GOING well in my life is my English paper proposal. It's the only assignment I'm doing. In it, I'm claiming the Minotaur is a rightfully angry victim of tragic circumstances, not a monster. Though I'm now pretty convinced victims of monstrous guardians are destined to become monsters themselves.

Look at me. I've practically become my mom.

Ms. Cole gives me the go-ahead on it. *Good premise*, she says in an email, *though I think there's a case to be made that there's a bit of a raging monster in all of us. Watch you don't paint yourself into a corner. Also watch for typos. At several points in your outline, you said 'I' instead of 'it'. Or are they typos? Subconscious ideas, per-haps? Are you okay, Kelsey? Feel free to get in touch anytime. I can connect you to a counselor if you'd like. Times are tough — please know I'm here for you if you need me.*

I'm good, I lie, embarrassed, *but thanks for your concern.*

And then I go back to sleep.

THE RAT-SCRATCHING AND parental yelling and neighbor battles are all too much for me one night, and after I pop a couple pills (one pill's no longer doing it), I decide I need some air. So I bun-dle up and head over to the playground at the local elementary school, stepping extremely carefully. All I need is to slip on some black ice.

The playground was being renovated before the winter, but the work wasn't completed. All the equipment's been demolished and carted away. The replacements won't come till the spring. Least there's nothing I can hurt myself on.

I stop at the foot of the playground path, and notice Ditch Gang Guy at the other end of it, smoking. He waves when I catch his eye, and gestures me over. I step gingerly.

"Hey," I say when I'm finally a few feet away from him. Don't want to go closer — I'm not masked and neither is he. I don't introduce myself — feel like that would be weird since we've been communicating silently for the past couple months.

"Hey," he says. He's lost a ton of weight. He was always slim, but had a lean, muscular kind of bod. Now he's heroin-shooting-musician thin. And his dark hair is long and greasy and hangs in his eyes.

"You're new at Queen," he says.

"Yeah."

He brushes the hair out of his eyes and looks at me. "What do you think?"

I shrug. "Same as every high school."

"They're like prisons," he says.

"Yeah, in a way."

"Can't wait to get out," he says. "To learn for real, you know?"

"Yeah, same."

"Freedom. Where you wanna go next year?"

"UBC's my top pick. Hope we get to go. You?"

"I'll have to stay in town," he says. "Weird family shit."

"Sorry."

He shrugs.

"I have weird family shit too. Hope I can get away from it. But that'll only happen if I get a scholarship. And if we have school by the fall."

"Hope so. Don't think I have the marks for a scholarship. Hard these days."

"Yeah."

We stand in silence for a bit.

"Got any food?" he says suddenly.

"No, sorry."

"I'm starving." He's shivering. "Sure you don't have anything?"

"I promise if I had some, I'd share." Actually, no I wouldn't, 'cause of the virus.

"Yeah, okay. Sorry."

I'm feeling sleepy now. The pills, the night air. I bend my head back and close my eyes. The melody of a popular song starts to run through my head, and I hum it. For some reason, I don't feel self-conscious around Ditch Gang Guy.

"Feed me," he whispers.

"What?" I say, straightening and opening my eyes.

"It's the lyric. And the title."

"Oh," I say. "Yeah."

There's a bit of a wild look in his eye now. Why did I come over here? I don't even know this guy.

And I'm feeling really strange and … slow.

I might die here, I think. And … I'm okay with that.

"I get it, but I want to live," he says.

"What?" I say again, startled.

"You said you're okay with dying. I get it, but I want to live, no matter how painful life gets. I think I can help you."

I didn't think I said that out loud. I also think he wants to … help me die. By … eating me? Like the Minotaur? That can't be right.

And then something occurs to me. "What if the pain doesn't go away?"

Now it's his turn to say, "What?"

"What if, when you die, you're stuck feeling whatever you're feeling at the time of your death? You could be in pain for all eternity!"

"I don't think that's how it works," he says. "Feelings end when you die."

"You don't know that! No one's ever come back! There are scientific explanations for tunnels and white lights! Oh god, I don't want to die!"

I back away. I can't have this guy eat me. "I have to go. I don't think I should stay here."

I take off, and when I round a corner of the path, I see he's trying to come after me, but he's in even worse shape than I am. He calls out a few times, but gives up after a couple minutes. And a couple minutes after that, I'm home.

I stumble into bed, shut my eyes, and everything goes black.

26

Ditch Gang Guy's slowly backing away from the bed.

Don't go, I want to tell him, I'm sorry I was weird, I have no other friends …

Molly's face fills the sky above my bed. She smiles and shakes her head at me.

Then Mom's at the end of my bed in a goalie-type stance. Dad's on the side, holding a clipboard and studying it. I wave at him frantically, trying to get his attention — I want him to get Mom to move out of my way so I can get up and go, even though I know I can't.

He doesn't look up.

A cage suddenly pops up around my bed and Mom smiles. She's got me — there's nowhere I can go, even if I could move. Then she whips a lighter out of her pocket, laughs, lights it, and says, "Burn it all down!"

"No!" I yell.

"You wanted to get rid of the rats!"

"But you'll kill all of us too!"

She laughs again and waves the lighter around teasingly.

Think!

"Shit!" I hear Mom exclaim suddenly.

Omigod, she's dropped the lighter.

I'm instantly surrounded by smoke and flames.

The smell is overpowering, and I'm coughing.

Dad finally looks up and sees what's going on.

And takes off.

Nice.

Shit. It feels so real …

Dammit! I can't wake up! Goddamn sleep paralysis! I order myself to stay calm and wake up right now …

27

AND IN A MINUTE, I do … to the sight of a giant rat on my duvet, staring at me.

I'm momentarily paralyzed in real life now, but then I spring into action and bash it with the giant bottle of lavender-goji berry essential oil I stupidly ordered from Doc Ashley that time. The smell of which is not even remotely pleasant — especially when mixed with the scent of freshly-murdered rat.

And now ew, there's a bloody, half dead mess on my bed.

Needless to say, I'm fully awake now.

And able to register the unmistakably real smell of a burning house.

"Shit!" I shout, and spring out of bed, having the presence of mind to quickly grab my phone and laptop off my desk. My door isn't shut all the way, and the hall's a bit smoky, but it looks okay to get out. Mom's bedroom door is open too, and I see flames starting to lick up the walls of her room. Fuck her and Dad too — why didn't he ever just take away her weed and ciggies and matches?

She's not in her bed!

Must be in the bathroom.

And Dad's in his room ...

"Mom! Dad! Run!" I scream at the top of my lungs, pounding on the bathroom door, then the door to Dad's room.

In a second, they're both stumbling behind me, looking confused — Mom 'cause she's out of it, as usual, and Dad 'cause he was obviously asleep.

"Move!" I scream so they'll pick up steam, and I run to the front door, hoping they'll follow.

As soon as we're outside, I call 911.

THE FIRE DEPARTMENT ARRIVES pretty quickly, and they manage to extinguish the flames before too much damage is done. It's mostly confined to Mom's room, but they can't let us back in until an inspector gives us the okay, and they can't get an inspector in until tomorrow.

A few of our neighbors came out to see what was going on — most to snap pictures on their phones. The screamers from next door glared at us, then took off. Only one person stays after Mom starts swearing a blue streak and Dad yells at her to shut the hell up because this is all her fault.

The lady approaches my dad in a lull and says we're welcome to stay in her basement. It only has one room and a small washroom, but it has a sofa bed and she has a couple of air mattresses.

What a sweet woman. She has absolutely no idea what she's getting into.

Actually, I guess she sort of does, having just heard that argument. Maybe she's an actual saint.

I almost want Dad to turn down her offer and say we're going to a hotel (or motel — probably all we can afford), but instead, he mutters, "Thank you. That's very kind. We'll take you up on that."

He introduces her to Mom, who enrages me by snickering and saying, "Wow, would you look at that — we ended up in Mr. Rogers' neighborhood." But even she (sober now) seems to realize that's over-the-line bitchy under the circumstances, and mumbles, "Thanks for the offer. Appreciate it."

Dad gets the head firefighter to promise to bring an inspector by at ten the next morning. Then we follow the lady, whose name is Christina, to her house, a couple doors from ours. There, we meet her wife Mika, who gives us all masks. They're both so lovely — the gay version of Molly's parents. Their daughter Hazel and son Elijah — both high school age, we learn — don't emerge from their rooms.

"They can sleep through anything," Mika laughs as she shows us to the basement — a time-warp-y, paneled job decorated with inspirational posters, one with a cat hanging from a bar and the words "Hang in there!" at the top.

Mika helps Dad blow up the air mattresses, giving Mom, who I'm pretty sure has a pill stash in her sweatpants pocket and has snuck one or three (she's spaced again now), the occasional puzzled look.

Dad thanks her in a tight voice when they're done and refuses Christina's offer of cookies and juice. Once they go upstairs, he lays into Mom, and I want to sink into the floor because Christina and Mika and Hazel and Elijah can absolutely hear the screaming.

Which rages on for an hour.

28

Hey, hi, so sorry haven't been in touch

M!! So glad to hear from u!! How are u? Ugh, awful, I know. Don't know what to say…

Was in a really bad space for a while. Still am. Can't believe she's gone & it's terrible with my dad & his gf

I'm so, so sorry, M. Anything I can do?

Would luv to see u (despite chronic introversion, lol) but can't now, 'course

I know. Everything sucks. Phone or Zoom call sometime?

Ya, maybe

Was there a funeral?

She had to be buried there. Only a few people went. Watched from here. Didn't feel like a real funeral so I didn't ask anybody here to watch. Will have a memorial sometime

Omigod, that's awful. Feel so bad for u...

TX, luv, how r u doing?

Ok xcept for the fact that I might have a lil drug issue + my mom just burned our house down

WHAT

Aw, don't worry. She did start a fire, but I don't think it all burned down. Will find out tomorrow. At a neighbor's house rn

Omigod, K!! U all right?

Ya. Just gotta hang on till uni, right?

If we get to go...

We'd better!

My mom dying was bad enough, but not knowing what's up the road is bad too…

I know. (Hence the drugs …)

Nooo K, u gotta be okay, luv u too much

Aw, same – will b okay, don't worry

How's school?

A shit show, nobody knows what they're doing

Ugh, I'm back to R virtually

Am here for moral support!

TX K, glad I have u 🖤

Same 🖤

29

I DON'T SLEEP A wink — even after Mom and Dad finally stop arguing and konk out. Both of them are snorers, but also, I'm too geared up and too many thoughts and feelings are racing through me. I'm so thankful and relieved Makayla's okay. Where the fire's concerned: rage, embarrassment, gratitude. Confusion about my feelings for my parents. I settle on: they're hard to love, but I'm glad they're not dead. (Also, did that thing with Ditch Gang Guy even happen? It sure felt real. But I guess I'll never know ...)

In the morning, at Christina and Mika's breakfast table, I almost wish we'd perished in the fire. Mom's her usual silent self, and Dad can barely look our hosts in the eye. Hazel and Elijah race out, having clued in to the fact that we're a horror movie family, and it's left to me to answer Christina and Mika's polite questions.

There's juice, coffee, granola, yogurt, and fruit on offer — *like a hotel*, I think — but I barely touch it.

As soon as he's eaten a bit, Dad tells us it's time to go and thanks Christina and Mika for their hospitality. He tells them he's sorry we were all on edge — it's not who we are. Haha, it so is, and they must know that, living two doors away from us, but they look relieved. Maybe they think the fire will catalyze some sort of change in Mom. That's something that crossed my mind too, even as I'm certain she's popped a bunch of pills since it started.

But I don't dare let myself hope for too much/anything.

"It isn't quite ten yet," Christina says. "Isn't that when the inspector's coming?"

"I'd like to … gather my thoughts and get some questions together before they arrive," Dad says.

Luckily, we don't have to sit and stew in our resentments — outside, in the freezing cold — for long. The inspector shows up ten minutes early and brings us in when he's done. "It's not too bad," he says.

The walls in Mom's room are grayish and there's some water on the floor from the fire hose. And a strong lingering smell of smoke. The inspector tells us we're lucky there doesn't appear to have been any electrical damage. He also tells Mom and Dad they'll have to sleep in the living room or basement until we get a restoration person in, and we should do that right away or we might get mold from the water, and have we contacted our insurance company?

Dad doesn't tell him he has his own room, that it'll just be Mom relocating, or that we don't have insurance (that's a guess on my part), just thanks him and says goodbye. Then we're left all by ourselves in our damaged house.

The metaphor seems a little too on-the-nose.

I escape into my bedroom, and when I go to the can a half hour later, I see Mom in her room — the door's half open — holding a bag of her stuff. She looks about to say something to me, but decides not to. Instead, she just swishes past me and heads down to our basement, which is unfinished and scary.

Another apt metaphor.

AGAIN, I DON'T DARE hope for any kind of real change — the popular pandemic term "hope porn" has become a fave — but I figure I have to strike while the iron's hot. Or the wall is charred, as it were. So later in the day, once Dad's cleaned up the water in Mom's room, I suggest another intervention. I got this idea after dreaming, when I finally got to sleep after a major episode of paralysis, that Dr. Drew broke down our front door and dragged Mom into his waiting Mercedes.

"She might not care what either of us has to say," I tell him, "but maybe she'll listen to somebody else." Providing she hears them. But the screamers next door haven't come back yet.

He doesn't answer right away, just looks at me. "Who?" he asks finally.

Wow, he's actually listening. But now I've arrived at the tough part. Who, indeed? Mom doesn't talk to any of her siblings, and she's alienated all her friends.

"Dave?" I suggest.

Dad shakes his head. "Her agent? She won't let him in the house."

Yeah, once you crossed my mom (as Dave did, in her mind, for suggesting she needed help), that was it for life. "Well," I say, "we should probably … surprise her." I don't want to scare her with the word *intervention*.

After a second, he says, "I don't know that he'd even do it." But after another pause, he says — to my shock — "But I'll ask him anyway." With that, he gets up, kisses the top of my head (!), and takes his dishes to the sink.

WHEN I COME TO the kitchen to make a sandwich for dinner (I'm sick of snack food), Dad tells me to go put a mask on, that Dave's coming. After I do and come back to the kitchen, I see Dad and Dave there, both masked. Dave does the virtual hug thing when he sees me, putting his arms in front of him in a circle.

"Mom's napping," Dad says. "I'm gonna tell her to come for dinner."

Haha, we'll see how that goes.

Sure enough, a couple minutes later, Dave and I hear Mom yelling about how she doesn't fucking want any dinner, but Dad says (in a strained, upbeat tone I've never heard before) he has a surprise for her. Once she finally agrees to come up from the basement, I head to the living room. I don't want her to see me. Yet, anyway. Feels a bit cowardly, since this whole thing was my idea. But screw it. I'm only seventeen.

'Course, she starts screaming at Dave the instant she sees him.

"Hannah, buddy, ya gotta lay off it all," Dave says when he can squeeze in a second of airtime. "You scared your hubby and kid to death. You coulda killed them."

My mom goes off on him again. "You think you're better than me? That's bullshit. You trashed my career!"

"Hannah!" my dad says sharply.

"What? You on his side now?"

"There are no sides, Hannah! We're trying to help you!"

"Yeah, by ganging up on me. Nice."

My dad doesn't answer for a few seconds. I sense he's trying to stay calm. Finally, he repeats, "We're trying to help you."

"Who says I need help?"

Dave says, "Hannah, you're past the point of being able to see it yourself."

"Melnick prescribed those pills to help me!"

"He shouldn't have, and he doesn't know you're taking more than you're supposed to," Dad says.

"You spying on me now?"

Please don't tell her it was me who figured that out.

"Hannah, stop it," Dad says.

"Stop what? My back pain? Wish I could."

"I guessed about the pills," Dad says. "Looks like I was right."

Thank you.

She just lays into Dave again. "Why're you really here, Dave? Did you want to get into my pants back in the day? Pissed it didn't happen? Want to make me look bad? You have some bloody nerve."

"You know I was never anything but professional, Hannah. And you also know you shot your own career in the foot. I'd be happy to help you find jobs again if you were committed to working, but right now, you're not hireable."

"Yeah, sure you would," Mom mutters.

"Hannah, that's enough," Dad says.

"Ya think? Dave hung around me for two reasons. One, so a little of my fame would rub off on him —"

"Because you were so famous," Dad mutters.

"See? That's what goes on here! That's why I need the drugs!"

"That's *not* what goes on here! Till you send us over the edge and we have to strike back!" Wish he wouldn't have said "us" that time. "And that doesn't even make sense! Dave's an agent! He works with dozens of famous people!"

Mom ignores him and says, "The second reason he hung around me is he had a thing for me."

"I said that's enough, Hannah!"

"Whaddya say, Dave? Still gonna deny it? It's the truth, right?"

"Hannah, you wouldn't know the truth if it bit you in the ass." Uh-oh, Dave's had enough. Which leaves me feeling a little panicked, and now I completely regret the whole intervention idea.

"You know what?" Dave says. "I can't do any more here. Sorry, Mark."

Dave heads to the front door and spots me out of the corner of his eye.

I shrug (*thanks for trying*). He nods back and says, "She was really good. You know that, right?"

"Yup." I've seen her pre-*Those Crazy Comics* stuff.

Dave nods and gives me a little salute, then walks away. Then my dad's at my side, saying, "I can't talk now. Have to go back in there."

I swallow. "Want me to come in?"

He sighs and says, "I don't know."

Right. Leave it up to the teenager.

Till now I've been hopped up on fire-related adrenaline, but suddenly, I'm exhausted again.

30

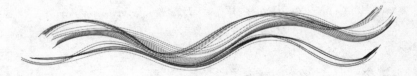

My mom's hovering. "Now who needs an intervention?" she sneers.

Suddenly, Dave's at my bedside too. "Hurry," he says to me. "You're going to be late."

I want to ask him for what, but I can't. I feel panicked.

"She's no actress," Mom sneers.

"I had such high hopes," Dave says, disappointed. He shakes his head and disappears.

Enter Christina and Mika, looking at me pityingly.

"You'd better come with us," Christina says tenderly.

I want to tell her I'd love to, but I can't.

"Why won't she come with us?" Mika asks her.

"Not sure," she says, frowning.

I try to tell them again, but I can't.

"You don't want her anyway," Mom — still there — says. "Nothing but trouble."

I'm trouble? I want to scream.

"Really?" Christina says, surprised. "I never would have guessed."

Don't believe her, I want to say.

Christina and Mika shake their heads and disappear.

"You think you're so smart," Mom says, grinning evilly.

Enter Dad. "What's happening now?"

"Your daughter's making trouble again," she says.

No I'm not, I want to yell.

"I've had it with both of you," Dad says, and then he's gone, leaving me with Mom, who's bending closer and closer and closer.

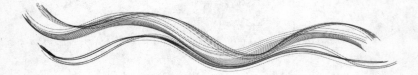

I make myself wake up, even though I'm well aware my waking life isn't that much less miserable than my sleeping one.

31

OKAY, HE'S STILL VERY far from being Dad of the Year, but at least the fire seems to have jolted him into action. A couple days after our laughably unsuccessful intervention, he comes out to the porch — I've stepped out for some air — to tell me he's rented an apartment nearby for us and taken a job in the communications department at an insurance company. A friend helped him find it, and he can do it from home. It takes me a couple minutes to figure out he's — we're — leaving my mom.

"I just told her," he adds. "She's pretty upset."

Which is code for she's ranting and raving so I shouldn't go back inside yet.

His news is both great and terrible.

I wanted to leave in the guise of leaving for college. Why couldn't he have waited till then?

Never mind. I know why. And I can't really fault him for it. We all could have died.

"I'm going in." I'm pretty sure she'll just scream at me for going with him, but if she does, well, I guess that'll make doing so easier.

He looks concerned.

For good reason. She does, indeed, go off on me.

"You going too?" she roars. "Nice. Leaving me all alone. You know what? Good. Go. Get the hell outta here."

That kills, but also alleviates any guilt whatsoever I have about going with Dad. Not that I'm dying to live with him either. "Get help," I say. "So you can live with people again." Not that she was ever easy to live with.

She doesn't respond, and I feel a little better.

Maybe she realizes I have a point.

OUTSIDE ON THE DAY of the move, Dad hugs me awkwardly when I start to cry. More over the mother I never had than the one I do have. After a minute, I ease out of the hug — I'm still upset with him for putting me in the position he's put me in — but follow him to the car.

THE NEW PLACE IS one of those old brown brick buildings with no lobby.

But the unit itself is painted white, and it has a bunch of big windows and a balcony. Dad's had some cheap living room furniture delivered. He got a sofa bed because it's a one-bedroom. He insists I take the bedroom, says teens need their space. He tells me the sofa bed is super comfy. That feels like a lie, but I'm grateful. He's trying. And I don't plan on being here long, anyway. Although there's still the very real possibility that the virus might upend all my plans for the next year or two.

Dad introduces me to (the masked, as are we) super, named Simon. He's an older, male version of Chelsea — super chatty. "Hey, Kelsey, good to meet you." He says he's spent the whole day cleaning and disinfecting the place. Right now, he's fixing a leaky faucet. "I was telling your dad earlier, you have any problem at all, just give me a ring. I live to fix stuff. Any questions before I go?"

"Yeah," I say. "Are there rats in this building?"

Simon laughs. "Nope. No rats or mice. No bedbugs either."

"That's good," I say. "And the smoke alarms work?"

Dad looks a little embarrassed. Tough.

"Tiptop," Simon says, looking at me and then at Dad, who doesn't meet his eyes. "Is that it?"

"Yeah," I say.

"Okay then. All the luck in your new home."

We'll need it, I think as he leaves.

I TEXT MOM A simple *How are u?* that night and she replies *Fine*.

I can't stand not knowing what we are, what we're going to be like up the road, but I tell myself it is what it is. She's a lousy parent; I have nothing to feel guilty about, and I — the kid — certainly shouldn't be the one doing all this emotional labor. I'll text her every few days, and if she's decent at some point, I'll consider visiting. Until then, I have to try to just not think about her. The same way I never think about Luca Kitescu.

Hahahahahaha.

I'm shocked when, later that night, while checking my Insta feed, Mom's name pops up. She's suddenly active again after a two-year hiatus.

She's posted a family picture. Of the three of us at a summer resort ages ago — a trip I actually have fond memories of. A lone heart emoji is the accompanying message.

Huh. Maybe we actually do mean something to her.

And maybe (dare I even hope?) the intervention and move weren't entirely unsuccessful, after all.

32

Omigod, K, now my dad's sick – think I gave it to him

Omigod, M, I'm so sorry! Is he in the hospital?

No – he can still breathe. But so could my mom till she couldn't. I'm so scared – I must've been a carrier. We left before I could get tested, & I didn't think about testing here, was so messed up, & Dad & Hayley "don't believe" in the virus (don't even believe Mom died of it, ffs!) so they never suggested …

Not sure who can get tested now – get if u can, but was probs not u!

Hayley's blaming me even tho she doesn't believe in it!!

Was probably her!

What if he dies? How will I live with that?

He won't, sweetie. He's in good shape

So was my mom

Is he staying in his room?

Ya. We're leaving food & drink at his door. But he's super tired like my mom was

He'll be okay, M. Make him drink a ton and take Tylenols

Will. Glad I have u to talk to

Call me ANYTIME

Again, hate the phone, lol

I know! Happy 2 text 2!

Heard some guy from ur school's sick too – weird, thot young people weren't supposed to get it

Didn't hear – who?

Don't know him. Name's Ben. Gorski, I think

Will check. Don't know 2 many people

Gotta go

Take care, M and remember – u can call or text me ANYTIME ♥

Will do – u take care too ♥

PART THREE
Oh God, It's Nowhere Close to Being over
—
(But There Are Tiny Glimmers of Hope ...)

33

THE GUY AT MY school who's sick — Ben Gorski — is none other than Ditch Gang Guy! I find and follow him on Insta. He follows me back, and I send him a DM saying I hope he's okay. He sends me back thumbs-up and wink emojis. I worry for a bit that I might have caught C from him that night at the playground, but I remind myself we were outside and at a safe distance, and it's been a while.

Makayla finally gets a test, and she's positive, though asymptomatic. But her dad makes a quick recovery and is well long enough that she trusts he'll stay well. I'm so relieved. Can't imagine what it must have been like, thinking he might die because of her. On top of her mom's death. Predictably, Hayley the girlfriend has taken off. Hopefully, M will be able to heal the relationship with her dad.

I have more hope for her than me.

In other news, there's talk of vaccines being developed, which makes the future seem not quite so bleak and unknowable.

By May, some businesses open up again, though school's still virtual. Ruth sends an email to all of us saying Soft Spot will be opening up again soon, and people are very excited about it.

Aw, her enthusiasm's sweet. Somehow I doubt we'll be that busy. (Many competitors, still-cold weather, people afraid to go out now ...)

I'm pretty nervous before my first shift back because I was so awful to the gang during the lockdown. Not that they'll all be there. Lee won't be back at all. He wants to work harder on his "brand." His TikTok reviews are still only getting about seven likes each, on average.

And Quinn is quarantining in preparation for filming Season One of *Never Fear: Quinn's Here!*

Wow, they even named the show for u! I say in a text. *Will u still talk 2 the little people?*

Only u, she answers with a wink emoji.

And Ruby's dropped off the face of the earth. Except she hasn't. When I ask in the group chat if anyone's heard from her, Quinn says she's been super busy since becoming president of her fan club.

What? U have a fan club? Even though the show hasn't even started filming yet? And are u 2 besties now?

Yes and yes. What can I say? Just knowing someone so pure gives me hope for humankind.

So it's me, Kira, Veer, and Chelsea when the store opens back up.

Ruth puts us all on together the first Saturday shift back, with a plexiglass divider between us and the customers and shields over our branded masks. There's a mask policy for customers too. We're also keeping a safe distance from each other behind the counter and keeping the door open so fresh air can circulate. Despite my fears about going back to work, I'm infinitely grateful I have somewhere other than my new home to spend time in. (Who'd have guessed, a couple months ago, I'd be dying to return to my crappy job?)

CHELSEA PRACTICALLY TAP DANCES when she sees me. And I suddenly realize that if someone's nice to everybody, that means they're nice, period. "I was so worried about you!" she shrieks. "You look amazing! Tell me everything! Veer, doesn't she look amazing?"

"She does," Veer says, smiling at me. At least I think he's smiling. It's hard to tell with masks, but his eyes are crinkled at the corners.

"Same," I say, looking back at him.

He's kind of cute.

"New flavor," he says, pointing from his spot to a container of blackberry soft serve.

"Big fan of sour fruit," I say.

"Sweet and sour — just like you," he says, and I laugh. Yeah, I'm sour as well as sweet. So is everybody. Like the Minotaur. I think Ms. Cole was right about that. I pray she still likes my paper.

Kira's a tougher nut to crack. She's cool to me. But I try. "I'm sorry about … everything," I say when Chelsea and Veer go downstairs to chop candy before customers arrive (we hope).

"It's okay," she says, but there's still a cool note in her voice.

"I know you were trying to help. I wasn't in any shape to accept it at the time."

"I get it," she says.

I hate this. She's still hurt, still afraid to be open with me.

I don't blame her.

But I'll keep trying. (Though I won't tell her I wouldn't go to a group even now.)

Despite the weirdness with Kira, it's great to be back.

Until an unmasked guy comes into the store, cursing at us for wearing masks and coughing all over the place.

But then Kira starts yelling at him and even comes out from behind the counter to sort of charge him, and it's kind of amazing.

"Hey," I say once she's chased the guy out, "you know what? I think you might be manager material, after all."

34

NO SLEEP PARALYSIS THAT night, but a dream. A nice one! Some-body bursts into Soft Spot to tell us COVID is over, and we can all take off our masks. We check our phones to see if it's true, and it is! Maskless people start to pour into the store, and everyone laughs and cheers and hugs and goes way overboard on their topping orders.

I'm kind of sad to wake up.

The virus is nowhere near over.

But at least I have some of my anchors back.

And I'll have to figure out how to be good with that.

35

"SOME OF YOU MAY know someone who's died by suicide."

Bolt's finally doing a synchronous health class with us —
they were just approved by the school board, now that the year's
almost over — and he seems even more uncomfortable on screen
than in person, but he gets points for not saying "committed,"
like suicide's a crime. "And others may know someone who's
attempted suicide. Some of you may even have thought about it
yourself." I don't think I imagine that he looks at me through the
screen for a split second. "Suicide is a permanent solution to a
temporary problem. It's the result of someone unable to see any
other solutions." He goes on to talk facts and myths about suicide and tells us loneliness is a big factor in depression. "You're not

alone if you feel lonely," he says. "Half of all North Americans describe themselves as lonely."

It actually helps to hear that.

And to recognize that, even though I never made a plan to off myself (I occasionally wanted to die, but more in theory than in practise), I've probably been depressed for years.

AND OKAY, THE VIRUS is still a thing — nowhere near over, as it was in my dream — but the fire flipped some kind of switch in me.

I'm done with drugging. Except for any anti-depressants I may — probably will — be prescribed in the future. It's definitely time to get my shit together. I don't want to burn my home down one day.

Online school sucks, as does the fact that a second wave of the virus is expected after the summer, but at least we have reliable Wi-Fi in the apartment, and I feel a bit more at peace here. I'm still hoping I won't be living with my dad very much longer, but even if my plan for next year crashes, at least I'll be living with just him and not her.

In addition to (gradually) cutting out the pills, I've vowed to start eating better. Dad and I have started taking turns cooking. He's not half bad. I'm a work in progress.

And I want to start exercising. For fitness and peace of mind. Re: the latter, I'm still skeptical about meditating, and I've given up on Doc Ashley. I've realized that self-help stuff makes me feel worse, not better. Like I'm not positive enough, don't visualize well enough, etc. Like my problems are all my fault.

Everybody's biking these days, even in bad weather, so I give that a shot on Dad's — and nearly die a dozen times when I take it for a spin around the block.

At a once-a-week boot camp class held in the park around the corner, I decide I'm not into being punished. I've heard enough yelling to last me a lifetime.

I decide I'll just walk more. I like walking. It's easy and low cost. And not only good exercise, but I've read it helps with depression.

Boom.

Over the next few days, I walk for hours, all over the city. And it does help.

But not nearly enough.

I MAKE A VIRTUAL Guidance appointment and get assigned to an older counselor — a Mrs. Wallace, dressed in a pink velour track suit — who spends a good five minutes of our session trying to figure out why her sound isn't working.

Of course I wind up with the one counselor even more techno-deficient than me.

I give her some suggestions — I've learned a few things — and finally, she gets it working. (She had another app open that was using the mic.)

"Thank you, dear!" she says. "So how can I help you today, Kelsey?"

Suddenly, I'm not sure where to begin.

"I think I want to ... talk about my life with someone." Okay, that told her nothing. Why didn't I practise this? I take a couple seconds to gather my thoughts. "I've been ... dealing with some stuff at home, and I think some of it might have affected me in a bunch of ways. I think maybe it would be a good idea to work through it with a professional."

I'm pretty proud of myself for what I think is a fairly good summation of my situation, but it's clear I've come to the wrong place. Mrs. Wallace looks super surprised and confused.

"Oh, I'm so sorry, dear," she says. "I mostly deal with scheduling conflicts and university applications. You're in Grade Twelve, yes? Did I see you in December? I don't remember you."

I almost laugh out loud. Has she not watched any Netflix movies for the past five years? The student mental health problem is epidemic. And Kids Help Phone has reported a fifty percent increase in calls since the pandemic started.

Ugh, I should have asked Ms. Cole to give me the contact info for whoever she had in mind that time. She probably knew Mrs. Wallace would be useless for personal stuff. "No," I tell her. "I was at a different school in December. I just applied to general programs at a few places." I pause. "Though I'm wondering now if that was a mistake."

"Many people do a general first year, then focus in on something afterward. Would you like to take an aptitude test?" she adds.

I say yes (what the hell) and spend the next half hour answering questions like, "What would you rather do: go to a party or stay home and read?" Who can ever answer these questions? Sometimes I feel like going to a party, and sometimes I feel like staying home to read.

Ultimately, the test decides I'm an extraverted introvert — whatever that is — and would make the perfect funeral parlor owner.

"Did you find that helpful?" Mrs. Wallace asks when I'm done.

"Not really, no."

"Oh." She looks perplexed. "Well, I'm sure we'll figure something out. Let's book another time next week."

"Mrs. Wallace, is there a ... social worker or a psychologist or someone who comes to the school that I can talk to about, you know, personal stuff?"

"Oh, yes. The next time he'll be available is —" she glances at a calendar "— the twentieth of June."

I almost laugh, but Wallace looks distressed and says, "That's quite far away, isn't it?" I begin to feel more kindly disposed toward her, even though she should probably be told her first words to a student in distress should be something other than, "I mostly deal with scheduling conflicts."

AT SOFT SPOT, I make ongoing efforts to engage Kira in conversation, though the store's slightly busier now. People are bored out of their skulls, and also, both Hotties and MERingue have gone under (the virus, plus legal actions re: the Hotties uniforms, plus the fact that vegan meringues taste like crap). Yet another new vegan dessert shop has opened in MERingue's old spot called tART, featuring mini tarts with wild flavors like orange creamsicle and cola. The space is decorated with art by neighborhood artists. This place, I'm guessing, might just survive. Which means we'll soon be in trouble again.

"Great hair. Love the blue."

"Thanks."

"Does Ruth have any plans to bring in hot beverages? Some of the other ice cream places do that. Since the big chains aren't in the hood yet, and Hotties is gone, the opportunity's there …"

"Not that I know of," she answers stiffly.

"She could also get customers to suggest ice cream flavors. This is such a diverse neighborhood. She might be losing opportunities by offering the same old, same old."

"Both good ideas," she admits — a little grudgingly. "I'll tell her what you said." She pauses, then says, "I've got some ideas of my own."

Yay — she can't resist me anymore! I knew it was just a matter of time. She's a sweetie. I implore her to tell me about her ideas, and now she enthusiastically describes them. Most of them are completely unworkable, given C-19 — celebrity appearances, live music performances, and the like. She also describes a bunch of ideas she has for businesses of her own. Doll hospitals! Mowing goats! She ends by saying, a bit bashfully, "You're the first person I've told any of that."

"Dude, I'm touched! And your ideas are so great!"

"Thanks. I'm glad you're back."

"Same."

She looks at me. "I know things are still rough for you."

It feels so good to have someone acknowledge this. Life with Dad is no picnic. He'll never be a TV dad — he's pretty messed up himself — and I'm still pretty lonely.

"Yeah," I say, not trusting myself with more words 'cause moist eyes.

"If you ever want to talk, I'm here."

"Same," I say.

And that gets her off on another monologue. Turns out she's been longing for friends too. Apparently there are several months she can barely recall, and when she went straight edge, she couldn't remember who her friends were. She asks if I want to hang out after our shift to talk (in a park, at a distance), and I think I might scare her off when I say yes so quickly, but she just grins from ear to ear and says, "Cool."

And then I think I really might cry because I've finally made another friend.

RUTH BUYS A FANCY espresso machine she (badly) teaches us how to use. On the advice of Kira and me, she's putting a variety of coffee-based beverages and hot chocolate on the menu. The machine's a big investment. I hope it pays off. And she's also taken my other piece of advice; in the store, we're now asking every customer for new soft serve flavor suggestions.

Fingers crossed.

OLD HABITS DIE HARD. Dad stays in the living/dining room when he's working and I keep to my bedroom. Maybe that's okay. There are all kinds of articles floating around about family members working in the same room and getting on each other's nerves. He does seem a bit more relaxed when we eat together. Even (gasp!) asks me the odd question.

Not that I'm quite ready to let my guard down and confide in him.

Le sigh. Baby steps.

I SEND MS. COLE a text asking her for that counselor's contact info, and she promptly gives it to me, saying if either of my parents has a workplace insurance plan, a majority of the fee might be covered, at least for a few sessions. And glory be, it turns out my dad has a plan now. Aside from answering my question about that in the affirmative, he doesn't say anything else about my desire to talk to someone. Nor does he say anything about how he should probably talk to someone too. Clearly, he thinks I'm the only damaged human in this apartment who needs help — aargh!

However, I do need help, and I'm not about to look a gift horse in the mouth, even if I half expect my appointment with the counselor (actually a psychologist) to be a disaster à la Mrs. Wallace.

But I turn out to like Cara a lot. She's young, and the first thing she says after she sees me enter her Zoom room is, "You look like you've been through it."

"It's … been a time."

She sends me a questionnaire to fill out, and it comes as absolutely no surprise when, after reading it, she officially diagnoses me with depression.

"TELL ME WHAT'S GONE on the last few months," she asks at our second appointment.

I do. About all of it — from my first day at Queen to today. Crying the whole time. (It's like a dam's burst …)

"Wow," she says while I blow my nose and wipe my eyes. "Well, first off, I want to tell you I think you're amazingly resilient. And resourceful. And I can also tell from talking to you just for this short amount of time that you're a warm and lovely person."

I tear up again. "Sorry. Nobody … tells me those things," I say. (Though I vaguely recall a couple nice things Chelsea and Luca said …)

"Well, they should."

She tells me about CBT — cognitive behavioral therapy — which will help me identify distorted thoughts and perceptions, and which we'll soon engage in.

I feel so much … lighter … when I sign off.

Also, suddenly I think I know what I want to do with my life.

I want to do what she does.

36

Organizing a Zoom memorial for my mom. U'll come, ya?

'Course! Such a nice thing to do, M. BTW, saw something on Insta – some magazine's doing online memorials for people who died from COVID. Can send link if u want

Would be great – TX! TX too for Cara's contact info – she's awesome!

Right? She's helped me so much, glad ur finding her helpful 2

So much

How's school?

Not so bad. For me, better than in-person, lol. And I'm extra paranoid about going anywhere now. Those vaccines can't happen fast enough …

Totally get it and hard agree re: vaccines

How's school with u?

Bit better now that they're doing synchronous classes – was lost without actual lessons

How r things with ur dad?

Not great, but okay – u?

Same

Stay away from soc media – all those pix of pandemic family bonding stress me out, lol

RIGHT? The family hikes …

The game nights …

The movie nights …

The baking …

Ugh, the baking, gag me

Lollll

WE WILL SURVIVE

DAMN RIGHT WE WILL

♥

♥

37

AS A KID, MY birthdays were always fraught. Every year, I managed to convince Dad I didn't want a party. Would have been too risky. The Mom thing, the possibility of no one showing up. Though, thinking about it now, I'm pretty sure most invitees would have come. I'm more the kind of person people are puzzled by, not the kind people actually don't like. In any case, at a certain point, Dad began to genuinely believe I wasn't a "party person."

I was a pro at coming up with celebratory activities that involved only me and whoever was glomming onto me at the time. Dad would give us money for pizza and a movie, or to go bowling or skating or whatever.

The no-party thing went on for so many years, I think even I started to internalize the I'm-not-a-party-person thing.

Suddenly, it occurs to me that not living with Mom means I can start inviting people home. Well, not inside yet (#COVIDLife), but the apartment has an outdoor courtyard. At which Dad won't hover. Because he's Dad, and also because suddenly, he's never here. He's immersing himself in a thousand and one outdoor extra-currics — boot camp, yoga in the park, cycling, etc. Making up for all the miserable years of staying home keeping Mom's secrets, I guess. Would be nice if he sometimes thought about doing stuff with me, but that might be too weird after a lifetime of not doing stuff with me. When we were living with Mom, on the one or two occasions he suggested we do something together, she got super mad. Further evidence, in her eyes, that everybody did her wrong — we were shutting her out, etc.

Over the course of my entire high school career, I was never invited to a single party. (Ha, can't believe I developed a drug problem without ever attending a high school party.) But thanks to Cara — and, if I'm being honest, Dad's example — I realize I have the power to make changes in my life.

It's finally time to determine whether I am or am not a party person.

I ORGANIZE AN OUTDOOR, distanced get-together for the Soft Spot crowd in the courtyard on a mid-May night when my dad's out. Kira and Chelsea arrive at the same time — Kira straight from work in her Soft Spot gear and a vest and Chelsea in a ginormous tulle skirt and green, faux fur jacket. (She's a real friend after all! She came to my party!)

"OMG, how great is this?" she says. There are a bunch of well-spaced Muskoka chairs in a circle in the courtyard, and I've put a pop can and small bowl of popcorn on each wide chair arm.

"Good to see you," Kira says. "We haven't been on a shift together for a while."

"I know," I say. "Miss you!"

"Here's Veer," says Chelsea.

Here is Veer, indeed. Looking rather spectacular in gray jeans and a leather jacket — unzipped, revealing an Easy Life tee.

"They're great," I say.

"Right?" he says, smiling.

Lee comes next. I invited him with the caveat that he wasn't ever to mention *The Wire* to me again. He laughed and said that would be super hard and he might fall down, but he'd try his best.

Then Quinn and Ruby arrive. Quinn picked Ruby up in the snazzy new car she bought with the huge pile of dough she's already made from filming (in a bubble with her cast and crew) the first half season of *Never Fear: Quinn's Here!*

Everyone peppers her with questions, and she holds court for a good ten minutes, then says, "Okay, even I'm getting sick of me. A little Quinn Pinkney goes a long way."

"Omigod," Chelsea moans when we're seated on the Muskoka chairs, and she eats some popcorn. "This is sooo good. Love snacks that aren't ice cream."

"Right?" I say. "Never thought I'd get sick of it. So," I add, "how did y'all manage school and stuff when everything shut down?" I'm curious to know how other people got through it.

"It wasn't too bad for me," says Lee, who goes to an alternative school. "We had a couple hours with our teacher on Google Teams every day, then we were on our own. I'm used to working independently, but it was stressful. Had a million projects. But I was glad to be busy."

"Same," says Veer, who's in a gifted program somewhere.

And I'm suddenly horrified to realize that I've been acting a bit Hannah-ish — failing to realize everyone else was as stressed and overwhelmed as I was. And that they may not have had the time or mental energy to check in with friends.

I don't ask Lee or Veer how they managed platforms, etc., since a) their teachers probably had time to answer questions, and b) they're both super tech-y.

"We had to do our spring show digitally," says Chelsea. "I was so looking forward to performing it live. It's hard to play off screens."

"I bet," I say. "I need live lessons. Thank god synchronous classes were just approved. Till now, school for me's been a disaster."

"Yup," Ruby says. She's at Queen's one-neighborhood-over rival school.

Kira says, "Glad I'm not in school. I would have flamed out in a pandemic." She pauses, then adds, "I flamed out even without one."

"Least they didn't allow our marks to go down," I said. "Though that radically reduced my incentive to work. I can't believe anybody did anything."

"Nothing else to do," Ruby says, shrugging.

"Yeah. Like Lee said, people were glad to be busy," Quinn said.

People who didn't start a busy career of pill popping.

"What did y'all get into, entertainment wise?" I ask.

"Lady Gaga," says Chelsea instantly. "*Chromatica* — so great, right?"

"*So* great," Quinn says.

I point to Veer's tee. "It's a couple years old, but I played *Nightmares* over and over."

"Dark," Lee comments.

"Dark songs can make you feel okay about your own dark stuff," says Veer, looking at me. "Or at least that you're not alone." I don't think I imagine another little moment between us.

I smile at him. "Exactly." To the others, I say, "But I'm not all about the dark stuff. I'm waiting patiently for Taylor to drop something. There are rumors."

"Circa Waves had a new album," Lee says, choosing to ignore the Taylor turn in the convo. "*Sad Happy*?" He looks at us expectantly, but no one responds. "Guess it was too much to hope y'all knew them," he says sadly.

"I read your review of it though," Chelsea says encouragingly. "Nice work."

"Thanks," he says, sighing.

Then Quinn says, "I take it you're all playing *Animal Crossing*?"

"The creators must have made a mint," I say. "Amazing timing."

"Omigod, I'm so addicted," Chelsea says.

"Same," says Ruby. "I play at least an hour a day."

Veer says, "Two," grinning.

"Three," says Lee.

"Four," Quinn says. "There's a lot of waiting around on set."

"What did everybody watch?" Lee asks. "Aside from *Tiger King*."

"What's *Tiger King*?" I ask.

"Seriously?" he says, and by the looks on everybody's faces, I guess it was a big thing I missed.

"About big cat zoos," Veer says. "Can't do it justice in a description. You've gotta watch it."

"Too campy for me," Lee says dismissively. "What else?"

"*Never Have I Ever*," says Chelsea.

"Never have you ever what?" I say.

Everyone laughs.

"It's another show," Quinn says, staring. "You been sleeping through the pandemic?"

"Basically, yeah." Now it's Kira's turn to send me a sympathetic look. "Haven't watched anything for a while."

Veer gives me a lovely I'm-here-for-you look, and I ask, casually, "How was it with your families?" This is the thing I'm really interested in.

"Bit too much togetherness," Chelsea says, "and I love my fam."

"Got that right," Lee says. "If I never play another game of Charades with my parents and brother, it'll be too soon."

"It's just me and my mom," Quinn says. "It wasn't bad. We like the same TV shows. I was in my room a lot, on calls."

Kira, who lives with Ruth, says, "Ruth's great, as y'all know."

This reminds me I should let Kira know again that I'm there for her too. There's obviously a story there re: her parents I've been too self-absorbed to ask her about …

Veer says, "My parents got on each other's nerves a bit. Wasn't fun."

Everyone murmurs their sympathy, including me. (Why didn't I ever check on *him*?)

"I think — hope — they'll be fine when they get more space from each other. It's been hard on a lot of families." He flashes me another sympathetic look. I think he suspects I'm in a bit of a different league.

I know he'd be a good listener if I ever wanted to talk about stuff. But I'm not sure how much I'd want to lay on him right off the bat. And I'm not even sure we should date, despite our connection — which I'm pretty sure I'm not imagining now. We'll probably be at different universities next year. Do I even want to start something up if I'm just going to lose it? Plus, there's the virus complication …

"It's true," Ruby says quietly. "I'm okay with my family, but my parents are crazy over-protective, and I have pretty high anxiety normally. It kind of goes off the charts when stuff like this happens."

Okay, now I really feel terrible.

"Join the club," says Quinn.

"Me too," Lee says.

"Seriously?" Ruby asks.

"Yup," Lee says. "Medicated and everything."

"Same," Quinn says.

"Wow," says Ruby.

"Aw, I'm so sorry, everybody," I say. "It must have been super hard for all of you, and I didn't even check in."

"I'm sure you had your own stuff," Veer says.

"I didn't check on anybody either," says Ruby. "I'm so glad everybody's okay. Luckily, I have a good therapist."

I hold up my pop can. "Me too. To good therapists."

She grins and holds hers up. "To good therapists."

Lee offers a second toast. "To learning to accept uncertainty."

"To focusing on the present and letting fears about the future go," Quinn says, and with that, she starts to belt out "Let It Go," and after letting her sing a solo line, everybody joins in.

At which point, she promptly stops. "Ugh, quit it, y'all."

It's so amazing to be having deep talks and joking around with friends (friends!). I kind of can't believe I made it happen.

I hold up my pop can again. "To making it through."

Everyone yells, "To making it through."

"And to friends," Chelsea says. (!)

"And new adventures," says Ruby. "Even though we can't really go anywhere to have them."

"To new adventures, even though we can't really go anywhere to have them!" everybody repeats.

"What's everybody up to this summer?" I ask.

"Oh, you know, just becoming famous," Quinn says.

"We'll see," Lee says, and Quinn sticks her tongue out at him.

"For those who don't know," I say, "Ruby's the president of Quinn's fan club."

"Oh, fun!" Chelsea says.

"Yeah, it really is," she says, her cheeks reddening. "I've started a blog, mostly about Quinn, but also about issues I want to write about and that the show's going to deal with, like anxiety."

"Ruby, that's amazing!" I say.

We talk for hours more. Near midnight, people start saying they have to go, and Quinn snaps a (distanced) group selfie. "For the 'gram!"

I can't believe I organized an event that'll result in an awesome Insta photo. And I have a hard time believing I'll ever pull off another night like this.

But weirdly, I have the strangest feeling I will again and soon.

VEER AND KIRA AND Chelsea leave. (Veer says what sounds like a very meaningful, "Later," before he takes off.)

While Ruby's on the phone with her mom, Quinn says she wants to tell me about something that happened to her a while back.

I had a feeling she had a story.

Turns out she was harassed by a perv-y teacher. It went on for a long time. And her parents weren't great sources of support.

"I get the feeling you've been through some shit too," she says.

I tell her I have and summarize my life.

She says, "Wow, I'm sorry. I've been talking to someone too — finally. Got tired of being an asshole. Turns out when you're abused, you start to see everybody as a threat. And you can get mean."

"Fight or flight," I say. "You fight."

"Right. "

"I'm a flyer. Don't allow myself to get close to people. Or I choose people who are unavailable. I've been talking to someone too."

"Listen to us, all shrunk and everything."

I laugh. "I'm so proud of us, trying to figure stuff out."

"Do you think we'll always be messed up?" she says after a second. It's the least Quinn-y thing I've ever heard her say.

"Yeah, probably," I say.

"Don't sugarcoat it or anything."

I laugh. "Just keeping it 100. I don't think it's a bad thing. Our experiences have made us deep, you know?"

"Ha, speak for yourself. I check out Gossip-Tok first thing every morning."

38

THAT NIGHT, I DREAM of another party, with older versions of ourselves. The older me feels happier than I do now, but I still have a sense of not being quite where I want to be.

I feel a little discouraged when I wake up. If there's anything that's gotten me through, it's the feeling that when I'm older, I'll have the power to make my life whatever I want it to be.

It wasn't real, I tell myself.

But, a second later I think, even if it was an actual glimpse into my future, well, I'll still be doing way better than I would have thought a few weeks ago.

And maybe that's just life. Maybe it will always have obstacles and challenges. It's about finding meaning, I think. Doing something good with what you've learned from hard times.

Chances are I won't be able to make my life *everything* I want it to be. Maybe I'll have to keep adapting or changing my dreams.

If I'm anything, I know I'm adaptable.

I'll be okay.

39

RUTH TOASTS ME WITH some cocoa a couple days later. Beaming at me, she says, "I'm so lucky you came to work at Soft Spot! Your ideas have helped me so much!"

Well, okay, I did help, but it didn't hurt that tART got shut down by the health department. Yet another new vegan dessert place has opened in its place, so Ruth's baby is probably toast.

Still, when she and Kira hip, hip, hooray me, it feels mighty nice.

DAD STILL BARELY PAYS attention to me, and I'm not sure I even want him to pay more — we're pretty different, and I'm not sure we'd get along even if we spent more time together.

Maybe he's trying to distract himself from his loneliness with busy-ness. Even though his marriage was crap, he was still with someone for a million (okay, twenty) years. And I know it's different living with a daughter than a spouse.

More likely is my theory that, having never known how to handle the situation with Mom — or me — he just removed himself from it and now the distance thing is habitual.

Ha, I'm definitely a future therapist.

He shocks me one night by saying, "Maybe I'll talk to someone too. About Mom."

It's not exactly a "Sorry," but it's something.

CARA SAYS, "HE MAY change, he may not. He may change for a bit, then revert to old habits."

"I'm still upset about how he handled things — or didn't handle them all those years."

She says, "You have every right to feel upset about that."

"That's good to hear," I tell her.

"You're definitely entitled to those feelings," she repeats, adding, "Could be he's trying to be a parent the only way he knows how."

"A generous interpretation," I say.

She laughs. "Agreed. But maybe life's a bit easier when we ascribe the most generous motives to people's actions. Which it sounds to me like you do, for the most part, even while knowing you deserve more."

It's nice to have my feelings validated and to hear someone say I'm generous. Even while suggesting I could do better too. Lol, I'm definitely catching on to her MO: validate my feelings, then slip in a practical suggestion.

"He did say he's going to start talking to someone too. About Mom."

"Well, that's good news anyway. Hopefully he'll learn something about his relationship with you as well as his relationship with your mom."

"I hope so."

"I do too, Kelsey. I really do."

SHORTLY AFTER MY MEETING with Cara, I meet — over Zoom — with April Britt, a peer tutor with a great rep, and tell her she needs to magically make me into an algebra whiz. Exams have been canceled, thank the universe — final marks will be based on course work and probably won't be forwarded to colleges and universities, but I'm not taking any chances.

She looks at me. "Not one of my clients has ever gotten below a ninety."

"Wow, really? This might be the first time," I say.

But I really hope it's not …

IN THE THIRD WEEK of May every year, Queen runs a program that pairs kids about to enter Grade Nine with exiting Grade Twelves, whom they can pepper with questions. I volunteer to be a buddy. Might as well start getting some mentoring/counseling experience on the resume.

"Hey, Ella," I say when I see her enter my Zoom room. "I'm Kelsey. Great to meet you."

"Hi," she says shyly. She reminds me of a younger me.

"I love your top." I really do. It's a cute blue puff-sleeved blouse. But I mostly say it because she looks self-conscious. I'm guessing she's wishing she wore something more casual. I pepper her with more compliments — on her hair and jewelry — then tell her to ask away.

"Thanks," she says, sounding super grateful. "I'll be coming from out of district, and I won't know anybody. I'm a little worried about ... making friends. Not that we're likely to have in-person school in the fall. But if we do ... did you make any new friends when you got there? In your classes? Ugh, sorry, I think I'm supposed to ask you other things."

"Omigod, no! I'm actually the perfect person to answer that question. I started here in January — I came from across town."

"Really?" Ella's eyes brighten.

"Really. And you know what? I didn't really make friends here."

"What?" Her eyes lose a bit of their brightness. "But you're so cool!"

"Haha, that's funny. For a long time, I trudged to a park ten blocks away for lunch. I got a part-time job at Soft Spot and made some friends there. Listen, sitting by yourself in the caf on your own some of the time or even all of the time is just fine. Trust me, nobody really cares." If school were back in session for real, I'd be taking my own advice. I have friends. I don't have anything to prove. And I have music and books and homework.

She nods, but I don't think she's convinced. "Listen," I say, "here's the truth. Even one friend is fine. Schoolwork will keep you super busy. You might find your people here. You might not. You might find them at your part-time job or somewhere else you hang out. You might not find your people till college. I'm hoping I find more there. But I might not find more friends till I start working after college. Whatever. We have all these ideas, from TV and movies, about what high school's supposed to be like and most of it's completely unrealistic. My advice to you is focus on finding things you like to do and on what you want your life after this to look like. You might not figure it out right away, but keep trying." I smile at her. "I didn't figure it out till right now."

AFTER OUR SESSION, I go out for a walk. All over the hood, deep in thought. And suddenly I find myself passing Luca and Angel on a sidewalk in front of an apartment building. His? He looks like he wants to go inside. I give them what I hope is a queen-like smile and slight nod. Angel nods and Luca shoots me a chin gesture.

Damn masks. I can't make out their expressions, but I think Luca looks a little shocked. Did he think he was never gonna see me again?

When I see him, my heart skips a beat, and I feel a little stab. But I recover quickly. Something in me's changed since talking to Cara, since having my party. I feel more … at home in my skin. Like I'm good enough. Way good enough. I still wish he hadn't flaked on me, but now I also think, *His loss*. (Also, I flaked on him too. Sure, he didn't answer those first couple texts, but over the next few weeks, I never tried again. He might've been over-whelmed and suffering too …)

They look and sound like they're arguing. Hmm, might she want him back? Is that why he's still looking at me? Has he remembered he wanted us to be together before the lockdown? Does he see what I now see in myself? Something … special? On some level, I think I always knew there were really good things about me, and now I constantly remind myself of them. I never want to forget again.

On another note, Angel's wearing an outfit she doesn't look at all comfortable in — a stiff jumpsuit and pointy-toed boots. It's something I might have worn in January when I was trying too hard. Today I'm in my now-standard uniform of sweatshirt, leggings and runners. (Why isn't she wearing sweats like the rest of us? We're in a pandemic!) I walk a couple klicks on the ravine trail near the apartment every morning, and my butt and legs look awesome. Plus, I can feel the self-confident vibe I give off. Eat your heart out, Kitescu.

Funny. I used to feel like everybody else led these charmed lives. Now I feel like I actually have a crack at leading one of those next year ...

"TIME FOR US TO talk about next year," Bolt says the next day in a synchronous class. "Hopefully, many of you will be living independently or becoming independent in other ways. What do you think you'll need to know and do to thrive? Anybody?"

"How to share a room with pigs," somebody cracks to laughter.

"How to share a room," Bolt corrects her. "Yes."

"How to self-motivate."

"Yes, good."

"How to socialize, but also have alone and studying time."

"Very important, yes."

"How to hold on to your priorities and convictions."

"Excellent."

"Finding a study method that works for you."

"Absolutely."

"How to reach out, ask for help," I say.

He gives me a big smile. "Now that's the big one."

40

Got into UBC! Have u heard yet?

Ugh, no, but congrats!

U WILL

WHAT IF I DON'T

Then u'll go somewhere else

WHAT IF I'M STUCK HERE FOREVER

Lol, dramatic, u won't be, I promise

Not a promise u can make, lol

Can! Ur marks were too good!

SO WHY HAVEN'T I HEARD

Know lots of people who haven't heard yet!

Lol, name one

Waiting, lol

OKAY I DON'T KNOW ANYONE
PERSONALLY BUT IT'S STILL EARLY

Not for scholarships

Impossible u didn't get a scholarship

Not

U have to get a scholarship &
come – won't survive without u

Lol, yes u will, u'll do great

Need u to explain humans to me

Lol, ur in trouble if depending on me

No way, u r so wise

U think way too highly of
me, but I appreciate it

U think way too lowly of urself

U will hear soon, guaranteed

From ur lips to god's ears
(if there's a god, lol) ♥

41

ITS MID-JUNE WHEN I get the notification from UBC. Even though I'm alone in the apartment when I read it, I let out a scream. I've been accepted with a full scholarship. (Which means I should have gotten notification earlier. Computer glitch?)

Sadly, it looks as though I might have to start or do the whole first year online — it doesn't look like there'll be a C-19 vaccine till mid-2021. But I'll get there eventually!

Of course I text Makayla first, and we scream together online. We'll be roomies whenever in-person school starts.

I text April before my dad. *Thank u, thank u, thank u!! Got into UBC with a full ride!!*

NP, is her businesslike reply.

Damn, girl, u r one cool cucumber.

Lol, congrats!

I can swing residence with a combination of a couple other scholarships I applied for that came through, plus money I've saved — and continue to save — from Soft Spot, plus an on-campus job and government loan.

I tell Mom via text and she texts back, *Good luck*, and I bawl for a good ten minutes. No "You deserve it" or "You worked hard" or "I'm proud of you" or "I love you" — all things another parent would say — but it's more than I expected.

I nearly drop dead when, a few minutes after I dry my tears, I get another text from her:

I'm in rehab/therapy. Dave hooked me up. Called him after you guys moved out. Also, he put me in touch with someone re: starring in a TV show about a messed-up actress!

Wow. It took her a while, but the fire and living on her own seem to have flipped some kind of switch in her too.

I start to visit her every couple weeks for about a half hour at a time. She carps about how little time I spend with her, and I feel guilty, but that's all I can handle, even though I can tell she's trying. She actually told me (once) that she loves me, which was good to hear. But I'm not ready to say it back. She hasn't done enough yet to earn my love. And I still don't quite trust her — even if I have the tiniest bit of empathy for her now, having walked a quarter mile in her shoes.

"I'm proud of you," Cara says. "You've set boundaries you seem able to live with. And she seems to be getting used to it."

At those words, I'm proud of me too.

FAST FORWARD TO OUR Zoom graduation. I'm happily surprised when Will Brown, of all people, keeps me entertained in a private chat with a running, snarky commentary on all the speeches. We agree we'll be extremely happy never to hear the words "pivot" or "resilience" again post-COVID.

Even with these new pandemic-related themes to draw on, no fewer than three of the adult speakers — our principal and VP and school trustee — quote from *Oh, the Places You'll Go*.

Oh my freaking god,

Will says the third time, *I'm sure someone besides Dr. Seuss has written a children's book people over thirty can quote at grad ceremonies! It's my junior high grad all over again!*

Haha, same!

Also, isn't Dr. Seuss canceled?

On a sombre note, there's a minute of silence for those who have died from COVID-19. And on an equally sombre note, the head of the Social Justice Club, Layla Smith, gives an impassioned speech about the Black Lives Matter movement that rose up in the wake of George Floyd's murder — which occurred between my meeting with Ella and my UBC notification. The Soft Spot gang and I attended Toronto's BLM march together (masked, of course) and started an anti-racist book club. I'm teary when Layla's done.

Then our class president, a smart and social type named Navneet Kaur, delivers their speech. It's a super emotional one about how we'll always remember the past four years as the best time in our lives and tell stories about Queen Secondary to our children's children.

Oh, hell, no we won't, Will says in our private chat.

Luca is our valedictorian. It's pretty torturous watching him speak, though he's movie-star handsome in his slim-cut suit. His speech is rambly and hard to follow. A literary star — a.k.a. a storyteller — would have been more likely to keep the audience entertained, which, in my opinion, should be the goal of the most important speech of the night. Not that I'm bitter or anything. Even though I'm about to receive the English Award.

About two minutes into the speech, Will says, *This is going nowhere fast. Love the guy, but this is a major snoozefest.*

Hope he hires a speechmaker when he wins his Nobel, I say. I might have dodged a bullet there. He might have bored me to tears.

After the Math Award is presented to Luca, Ms. Cole presents the English Award.

"The moment I laid eyes on the recipient of this award," she says, "I knew she was someone special. I saw something that made me suspect she had a keen insight into human behavior. She proved me correct with a series of creative and enlightening essays. One standout in particular gave a startlingly original take on the Minotaur myth. Today it is my honor to present Queen Street Secondary School's English Award to Kelsey Kendler, whose path in life I will be tracking with great interest."

It's such a beautiful and touching introduction, I tear up again.

"Congratulations, Kelsey," Ms. Cole says. "I'm so proud of you."

"Thank you," I say, unable to keep my voice from wobbling. "For everything." And I stop speaking so I won't bawl. My dad, sitting beside me at the computer, squeezes my arm.

"I'm so proud of you too," he murmurs. "And I know Mom is too."

She declined to come over to watch the ceremony, but she did say she'd come out to the walk-by cheering later. (We'll be in a distanced lineup in front of the school, and the parents will walk by in timed, bubbled groups and clap for us. Super weird but #COVIDLife …)

Next on the Zoom program is the diploma presentation. After each name, our principal also announces our plans for next year and any scholarships received. I love hearing my scholarship announcement.

Later, at the walk-by thing, I find myself standing (masked and at a distance) next to none other than Luca Kitescu. And Molly's on my other side, trying her best not to make eye contact — and to keep her parents from noticing us.

I'm infinitely glad I splurged on a super-flattering green dress that matches my eyes and spent a solid hour styling my hair. Not that I want to date Luca anymore. If I were to date anyone, it would be Veer, but I no longer need a boyfriend for validation. There's a whole new world waiting for me at UBC and a home-town boyfriend won't be part of it.

Luca says congrats to me in that weird, warm-yet-distant manner of his.

"You too," I say. "Great speech," I add. A lie, but I'm feeling generous.

"Thanks," he says. And I nearly faint when he says, "I'm sorry I — dropped off the earth."

"Hey," I say, trying to sound blasé about the whole thing, "we're all just trying to survive. I get it. And I should have kept checking in with you too."

He waves a hand and says, "So, *Happily Ever After*'s been canceled."

"Yup. After five ridiculously glorious seasons. Some things just aren't meant to be." Can't resist the dig.

Then the walk-by cheering begins.

After each (masked, spaced apart) family walks by the line, cheering and clapping, they join their kid from behind the line. My mom's actually here with my dad, in a sleek, black suit. She looks amazing. Like, Charlize Theron-level amazing. We don't get to talk right away when they join me because so many parents yell at her (through their masks, from a distance), "Big fan" or "Congratulations, you must be so proud!" Aargh. As if she's responsible for anything having to do with my accomplishments. I got where I am in *spite* of her. But I'm glad the 'rents are getting an opportunity to see what kind of kid they have. And — not gonna lie — I do feel a little swell of pride at Mom's appearance and behavior. Her star and mine are both shining brightly today. Wish it could be like this all the time.

Our exits are timed too. Something up ahead stalls us, and, bored, I make the mistake of looking behind me. So does my mom.

Oops, forgot Molly and her fam were beside us in the line and are behind us now.

And uh-oh, now Molly's mom, Leanne, looks about to say something to my mom.

I get the feeling she doesn't know why she never saw me again.

Molly looks hella uncomfortable. Like she'd rather be anywhere on earth.

"Kelsey," Leanne says to me, "congrats on everything!" She's a lovely woman. Knows better than to congratulate my parents first. I'm still hurt that Molly friend-dumped me, but I don't hold anything against her super sweet parents.

"Yeah, congrats, Kelsey," Molly mumbles.

I'm a performer's daughter. "Thanks."

"Leanne and Matt Jones," Leanne says to my mom. "Big fans of yours!"

Molly can't seem to take her eyes off my mom. I'm pretty sure she's trying to reconcile the unhinged woman she dumped me because of with the gorgeous, poised creature standing before her.

Despite the fact that it wasn't entirely fair to think badly of her, it still feels mighty good having the tables turned.

But of course, she knows what my mom's really about. (And I'm under no illusion I'll have another night like this anytime soon with Hannah.)

I don't think Mom recognizes Molly. For sure she doesn't remember what happened that day — she was so out of it.

Then again, maybe she does. Her eyes narrow slightly. A dim recollection?

Maybe not. To Leanne and Matt, she just says smoothly, "Thanks." So gracious. Such a good actress. Shame she blew up her career.

"Congrats from me too, Kelsey," Matt calls. And then, looking at my mom, "We loved you so much on *Those Crazy Comics*. What are you up to these days?"

After a split second of hesitation (during which I hold a breath), she says, "Oh, I've been taking a little sabbatical. Show business is tough, as I'm sure you've heard."

Leanne and Matt laugh on cue.

"My hiatus was pretty hard on these two." She gestures to me and Dad. "I'm not the easiest person in the world, as I'm sure was evident to you watching me on TV."

Leanne and Matt laugh again, a little nervously this time.

"I'm so glad Kelsey has a good support system," she continues.

"Real, solid friends to turn to in times of crisis, you know? Her work friends are amazing."

Molly looks slightly nauseated now, and understanding begins to dawn on the upper, non-masked halves of Leanne's and Matt's faces.

"Well, it was lovely to meet you," Leanne says quickly. "Congratulations again, Kelsey."

"Thank you," I say, turning back around. The line's moving again.

I'm kind of stunned. For a second there, Mom kind of owned her shit.

And she dissed Molly without outright insulting her.

It was kind of perfect.

I guess she does, in fact, have some Mama Bear instincts somewhere under there.

And omigod, I'm just now noticing that Luca — in front of me — heard everything. He looks a bit embarrassed too. (He didn't ghost me 'cause of my mom, specifically, and yeah, maybe I should have kept checking in with him too, but he *did* ghost me ...)

I give him a gracious nod.

He nods back, looking abashed.

It's kind of delicious.

SHE REALLY IS PROUD of me. She actually says it before we drop her off. "Proud of you, kid," are her exact words. Her voice is wobbly, and her eyes are teary when she says it. And I nearly drop dead of shock when she says, "I wanted to tell you both ... I'm sorry. I'm gonna get better." Then she leaps out of the car and runs up the steps of her new building. Heaven forbid she should express too much (any) emotion. Might explode or something.

At home, Dad gives me a quick hug and says, "I'm really proud of you too. I know this hasn't been … an easy year."

This hasn't been an easy life, I think but don't say.

And then, because he, too, is allergic to Feelings, he busies himself in the kitchen, and I sigh and head to my room to electronically debrief with my friends.

I'M FEELING SO STRANGE. Happy. Excited. I'm headed to uni! (Maybe. Hopefully. Even if it ends up being online, it's something.)

I open my computer to catch the news that Dr. Ashley and her Insta-perfect hubby, who's always described as a "financier," have been implicated in a massive pyramid scheme. Yikes. I'm infinitely glad now I never "spread the word."

I get lost down that Internet hole for a while, and then I decide to send an Insta-message to none other than Angel Aquino, who missed grad. And virtual prom too, I heard. I skipped that because I had no friends at school; she skipped it because she had — said the rumor mill — some kind of … episode. Now that I think about it, when I saw her and Luca that time, it seemed like she'd just reamed him out about something — probably for deserting her in her time of need, even if just as a friend.

Hey, how r u? Just FYI, anytime u feel like chatting, I'm here. I had a rough year 2.

She doesn't answer right away, and I feel terrible because I realize I probably offended her by making my message about me. *When will you learn?* I think.

But the message that comes a minute later is incredibly sweet.

Omigod, that is so nice of u! I'm sorry u had a rough year. How so? (U don't have to tell me.)

Well, the pandemic, obvs. And bad family stuff. Things are a bit better now. Hope ur in an okay space too…

Yeah. I buckled under the pressure. Some of it self-induced. Was happy I could help my family by monetizing my Insta feed, but took on way too much responsibility. And once my platform grew, the 'rents got a little carried away too. Also, Insta pressure is its own thing — dealing with trolls, never knowing if people like u for who u r or what u look like … which even isn't what u look like. And I'm not even as well known as other influencers. OMG, sorry!!! So much word vomit!!! Back to u, being the new kid is never easy …

No worries!! U had so much to deal with, wow!! And ya, I felt really out of it.

Really?? I envied u so much this year! Ur so cool and nice and pretty!

ME? I left school at lunch every day! And I felt the same about u!

Ha. It's all in the spin, baby. Hey, want to meet at Grand Electric in an hour? The patio's open.

Ur on.

And just like that, I have another friend.

Before I leave, I check a group chat some peeps assigned to my UBC residence floor have organized. Weirdly, Makayla and I were put on the psych majors' floor, even though I was too late with my career decision to specialize in first year. A sign I'm on the right path?

Somebody's posted.

Sooooo, since we're the psych major floor, I'm assuming we all come from messed up families and are mega screwed up, lol. Do we tell each other how much and the gory details now, or do we wait till we get to know each other better?

I look out the window as I think about how to respond. It's just rained, and it's foggy, but I think I see Ditch Gang Guy — Ben, I remind myself — on the street below my window. He looks better. Healthier. Happier. Like I do, probably. Haven't had any sleep paralysis for a while now. Ben's eyes are closed, and he's sticking out his tongue to catch raindrops. When he opens his eyes he sees me, smiles, and waves.

I smile and wave back, then turn back to my computer and type, *Sounds like a fine first-night talk fest to me ...*

ACKNOWLEDGMENTS AND RESOURCES

IT'S BEEN ... A TIME, amirite? It's my sincere hope that by the time you read this, the COVID-19 pandemic will be naught but a fading memory ...

For me, writing was a way of staving off panic during the lockdowns. When I write, thoughts of all else fall away. It's like a days-long mindfulness exercise — I become completely immersed in the world of my book. And I poured my heart into this one. As is evident from the dedication, I really felt for all the kids and teens who were stuck in crummy home situations during the lockdowns. I'm so grateful to those who helped make this book the best it could be so those kids and teens could see themselves represented in this fictional record of the first months of 2020.

Huge thanks to all who provided invaluable feedback on the manuscript: fellow teen lit writers Danielle Younge-Ullman, Maureen McGowan, and Alisha Sevigny; my wonderful agent Stacey Kondla at The Rights Factory and TRF editorial assistants Leah Reynolds and Tasneem Motala; and DCB's amazing publisher/ editor Barry Jowett.

Thanks, too, to the rest of the incredible team at DCB/Cormorant, including Sarah Cooper (Managing Director), Chantelle Cho (publicity), Sarah Jensen (copy editing) and Angel Guerra and Tannice Goddard (cover and interior design).

I've actually been playing around with Kelsey's story for years, so thank you, too, to those who critiqued the book in earlier, different incarnations: Joanne Levy, Maia Caron, Heather Wardell, and Danielle Younge-Ullman and Maureen McGowan again. (With fond memories of the writing group we all formed before any of us were published!)

On a personal note, I must extend an enormous, loving thank you to Andie Rosenbaum-Meade, Autumn Rosenbaum-Meade, Ricky Rosenbaum, and Brian Rosenbaum — the best and funniest C-19 bubble anyone could have.

To Dr. Karline Treurnicht-Naylor: thank you for everything. My gratitude is immeasurable.

And now. This book is about, among other things, depression and addiction. In this realm, I must acknowledge my debt to the works of Dr. Gabor Maté for their acute insights on childhood trauma and development, and stress and addiction, as well as the book *Adult Children of Alcoholics* by Janet Geringer Woititz.

The pandemic has seen rates of mental distress and substance abuse in teens (and everyone else) rise astronomically. Thank you to the *Toronto Star* and *The Globe and Mail* for publishing enlightening articles on these issues throughout the pandemic, which served as inspiration.

If you suffer from either depression or addiction, know you are very far from alone and there is absolutely no shame in reaching out for help. I promise it is available and things will get better. Here are a few resources:

CANADIAN

Kids Help Phone. For kids and teens. Call 1-800-668-6868 or text 686868 or visit kidshelpphone.ca.

Canada Suicide Prevention Helpline. Call 1-833-456-4566.

Distress Centres of Greater Toronto. Visit dcogt.com for resources, or call 416-408-4357.

211 Ontario help line. Call 211.

The Centre for Addiction and Mental Health. Visit CAMH.ca for support and information.

AMERICAN

U.S. Suicide Prevention Lifeline. Call 1-800-273-8255 or visit suicidepreventionlifeline.org for resources or a live chat.

U.S. Crisis Text Line. Text HELLO to 741741.

Mental Health America. Visit mhanational.org for support and resources.

Big love to all.
Bev

Bev Katz Rosenbaum is the author of the *I Was a Teenage Popsicle* series and *Who is Tanksy?*. She has taught creative writing at Centennial College and is an award-winning publishing industry veteran. Rosenbaum, a devoted coffee drinker and chocoholic, spends her downtime reading, baking, and watching movies. She currently lives in Toronto, Ontario.

We acknowledge the sacred land on which Cormorant Books operates. It has been a site of human activity for 15,000 years. This land is the territory of the Huron-Wendat and Petun First Nations, the Seneca, and most recently, the Mississaugas of the Credit River. The territory was the subject of the Dish With One Spoon Wampum Belt Covenant, an agreement between the Iroquois Confederacy and Confederacy of the Ojibway and allied nations to peaceably share and steward the resources around the Great Lakes. Today, the meeting place of Toronto is still home to many Indigenous people from across Turtle Island. We are grateful to have the opportunity to work in the community, on this territory.